UNDER THE
BRIDGE

UNDER THE BRIDGE

BY MICHAEL HARMON

Alfred A. Knopf
New York

THIS IS A BORZOI BOOK PUBLISHED BY ALFRED A. KNOPF

Visit us on the Web! randomhouse.com/teens

Educators and librarians, for a variety of teaching tools,
visit us at RHTeachersLibrarians.com

Library of Congress Cataloging-in-Publication Data
Harmon, Michael B.
Under the bridge / by Michael Harmon. — 1st ed.
p. cm.
Summary: Wearing a police wire, a skateboarding street boy from Spokane confronts the drug dealer who threatens to kill his brother.
ISBN 978-0-375-86646-3 (trade) — ISBN 978-0-375-96646-0 (lib. bdg.) —
ISBN 978-0-375-89642-2 (ebook)
[1. Skateboarding—Fiction. 2. Brothers—Fiction. 3. Drug dealers—Fiction.
4. Spokane (Wash.)—Fiction.] I. Title.
PZ7.H22723Und 2012
[Fic]—dc23
2011036368

The text of this book is set in 12-point Goudy Old Style.

Printed in the United States of America
November 2012
10 9 8 7 6 5 4 3 2 1

First Edition

For Syd and Dylan

Special thanks to the crew: my son, Dylan, Andrew, Keylen, Aaron, Morgan, Hoover, Litz, and all the other skaters and friends who have filled our home with laughter, love, half-pipes, band practice, great times, awesome stories, and craziness. Your duty, respect, trust, and friendship toward each other inspire me and helped me write this story.
This one's for you, guys. And for Snakebite!
With love and respect, Mike

CHAPTER ONE

"This is not a drill. Please exit the school to your designated target areas immediately."

I looked up at the intercom as the tired voice of Vice Principal Lackard echoed through the halls. If there was concern in that tinny voice, it was masked by complete indifference. Maybe a hidden wish that one of these times it would turn out to be real and that this school would end up being a shrapneled example of what went wrong with our youth. Of what went wrong with this world. "Such a terrible loss," he'd say, splaying his hands and shaking his head to the news cameras while behind him the smoking ruins of our fine institution collapsed upon themselves.

Then he'd go home, sit on his back porch, his wife would hand him a gin and tonic, and he'd tell her we deserved every last piece of rubble. You could see it in his eyes when he walked down the hall. Guys today don't shoot spitballs and gather after school for the occasional fistfight. They punch teachers, stomp heads, sell dope, pack heat, and make pipe bombs. I didn't blame the guy. We're pretty fucked up as generations go.

I walked from my locker, my pack over my shoulder and my board in my hands. No English today. I glanced at the clock above the exit as I shouldered my way through masses of students pressing for the doors; half of them bug-eyed, the other half accustomed to evacuations and looking forward to sixth period being cut from the schedule. I could hear the sirens already. This was becoming routine.

"Lemmings on the march."

I turned, and Sid, long black hair in his eyes, deck slung through his pack, skintight straight-leg jeans outlining his bony knees, sauntered toward me. We walked closer to our designated herding area. "Bomb threat, right?" I said, wondering if this one might be different. Alien invasion. The president visiting. Something to look at besides three thousand students streaming from the campus like water from a shotgunned and rusted barrel.

He grinned, looking back at the red-and-gray brick Goliath called our school. "Yep." Either Sid Valentino could hear the whispering voices through the walls or he was psychic, but he always knew what was going on in this place. And everywhere else.

"False alarm?"

His Adam's apple bobbed as he chuckled. "If we gotta dodge flying bodies in the next few minutes, I'd say real."

2

Sirens screeched closer from the downtown core of the city, racing toward the school. In the next moment, the Spokane City Bomb Squad rolled by in some kind of *Star Wars* armored vehicle, black-uniformed guys hanging from the sides, studying us like we might be the next Bin Laden. "This is lame," I said.

"Wanna hit the Monster? Piper and your bro should be there on this occasion of terrorist-inspired freedom."

Standard evacuation procedure said that once each group of the student body reached their "target" points, buses would transport three thousand students to the Veterans Arena, five miles away, for our parents to pick us up. Disciplinary procedures would be applied to any student leaving without a parental signature. Dad would be more pissed about having to leave work than about me getting busted for what he called idiocy. We could take care of ourselves, and Dad quit being our babysitter a long time ago. "Sure. I'm not wasting the next four hours sitting in a parking lot."

Sid smiled. "They're just grooming us to be good refugees. It doesn't work if nobody knows how to be refugee-ish."

I adjusted my pack higher on my shoulder. Sid wasn't exactly the most optimistic of people. "I can think for myself, thanks."

He loped along next to me. "Thinking is dangerous, dude. Just blindly follow. It goes along with the grand plan of devolution."

I laughed. "Whatever, Sid."

A good six hundred students milled around our staging-

and-transportation area as we arrived. Sid gazed at the crowd. "See, I'm right. Evolution in reverse."

I smirked. "How?"

He laughed. "When some dumb-ass calls in a bomb threat, our incredibly brilliant leaders evacuate a fifteen-acre school to avoid a large body count, pack us all into two areas that are a quarter the size, and call it a 'safe' zone."

"Yeah, so?"

He looked around. "I don't know about you, but I don't see much that makes this place safe, and I do know that any wacko with half a damn brain would call the threat in, wait till we're all packed together here, then blow us up. He'd need half the explosives to kill twice the people." He paused. "Devolution, man. And I don't know who's worse—the jackhole that came up with this plan or the idiots who follow it."

I chuckled. Sid might have been the most dark, depressing, moody person I knew, but his logic made sense. "I suppose so."

"I know so. Look. They think they're safe because some tardo told them they're safe."

"Well, I'm glad you're not a bomber."

He shrugged. "People are so good at killing themselves they don't need my help."

"True."

Sid nodded, looking around again. "I don't feel like being stupidized any more. Let's split."

I nodded. "Under the Bridge?"

He unstrapped his board. "Under the Bridge it is."

. . .

Under the Bridge is the one thing that makes Spokane even close to cool for teenagers, and when the city built it, we thought it would be the lame of the lame when it came to skate parks. A bunch of square-headed politicians sitting around figuring out how to get votes. They'd build a park, all right, but it would suck in the best politically correct way. Helmet and pads required. Rules. Regulations. Security guards. Shallow bowls and short rails. A homogenized version of what could be cool.

Wrong. Before breaking ground, the developers actually brought in a dozen boarders and talked with them about what makes a park a good park, and they did a hell of a job on it. They also built the Monster, and my brother, Indy, owns it.

The Monster is the biggest, deepest, craziest skate bowl in Spokane, and the state of Washington for that matter, and Indy skates it like he was born on the flip side of a deck. Sixteen feet of vertical concrete keeps the kiddies on the other side of the park, and we like it that way.

Indy's a year younger than me, and probably the best skater, sponsored or not, in the city. He's also the worst high school student in the universe, too, which pisses me off because he could ace every class if he wanted to. I, on the other hand, suck at school because it's hard.

He laughs when I tell him he could do better. Life is like

balancing on a teeter-totter, he says, and the trick is to get some big-ass air before the world jumps off the other end and smacks you down. That's the difference between us. I don't like teeter-totters; he jumps on them every chance he gets.

As brothers, he and I share a mother. And a father. A hugely muscled metalworker of a father who has a hard time knowing who he's yelling at after the school calls about Indy skipping class. I should get I'M JUST HIS BROTHER tattooed on my forehead. Dad's anger is like a bomb going off, and anybody caught in the damage zone is toast.

The Monster sits on the far edge of the concrete skate park, stuck between two of the dozen huge concrete pillars that hold the freeway up above our heads. Under the Bridge. Located just on the edge of downtown, it was almost like home to Indy, Piper, Sid, and me.

There's a three-foot-high concrete wall dividing the park from the street, and we meet there every day after school. As Sid and I reached it, Piper, kicking his heels against the wall as he sat, nodded to us. I unslung my pack, dropped it next to my board, and hopped up on the wall next to him, waving to Stumper the Bum, who half dozed in a drunken stupor next to his shopping cart across the street. Bums on this end of the park, drug dealers on the other. I wondered where Stumper would be when the end of the world really came, realizing that Sid had nothing on being a refugee. Stumper had been one for years. I slapped Piper five. "Seen Indy?"

"Nope. Not in class this morning, either," Piper said. Piper and Indy had second period together. He hitched a thumb toward the school, where we could still hear the sirens. "They should just plan these things. Make it easier on my schedule."

Sid hopped up to the ledge and shook a smoke from a crumpled pack of cigarettes, lighting up. "Only real people have schedules."

"And you're a real people?"

Sid hot-boxed the cigarette, his already hollow cheeks sucking in further. The bonus about thinking you'd die at any given moment was that lung cancer in fifty years didn't enter the equation. "Sure not. Wouldn't want to be."

I took a piece of gum from my pocket and stuck it in my mouth. "Not in class, huh?" I unzipped my pack and unfolded my report card, a reminder that another kind of apocalypse would be waged at our house tonight. I stared at the grades. Four B's, a C in math, and an A in fitness. I knew mine were better than Indy's, and I sighed.

Piper spit. "Saw him this morning in the parking lot. Figured he'd be here."

Sid glanced at my grades. "Can I have tickets?"

"To what?"

"To your dad ripping your head off and crapping down your neck."

I tucked the paper in my pocket. "Yours are better?"

He laughed. "My dad's passed out by the time I get home, Tate. I got no worries."

"What about you, Pipe?"

"Two B's, two A's, and two C's."

"Wow."

He nodded. "My mom owes me five bucks per A. We made a deal."

Sid rolled his eyes. "Sellout."

Piper shrugged, holding up his middle finger to Sid. "Know what this is?"

"An offensive gesture in fifty-three countries?"

Pipe shook his head, smiling. "Nope. Me not giving a shit what you think."

Sid clutched his heart. "Mortal wound."

I gazed around the park. "Indy didn't say anything to you, Piper?"

"No, but he's been hanging with Angie. And that new guy, Will. I saw them at lunch yesterday."

I watched as a few private-school kidlets, out early for some private-school reason, piled out of a minivan with their moms, apparently unaware that Lewis and Clark had been evacuated due to a bomb threat. My thoughts went back to Indy. He'd never been voted attendance king, but lately he'd been skipping more often. "Will? Tall guy? Shaved head with a tat on his neck?"

Sid nodded. "From Texas. And that tat is killer."

"He skates?"

Sid shook his head. "Naw. I heard he packs, though."

I grunted. "A pistol?"

"No, a pickle."

"Is he a gangbanger?"

"No."

"Then what?"

He shrugged. "Just hard-core. Nobody really knows."

Piper spoke up, his sandy voice droll. "Like thirty percent of all Texans carry guns. I read it in *Playboy*. It's on account of the beaners. The beaners and gringos don't like each other because of the Alamo."

I smiled. "Read that in *Playboy*, too?"

"No, but the Mexicans pee on our lettuce to get back at us," Piper shot back.

Sid shrugged again. "Ozzy Osbourne pissed on the Alamo. Got arrested."

Piper shook his head. "I'm serious. Ever seen a porta-potty in all those fields down south? Just a bunch of Mexican dudes peeing on our food because we put the *x* in Texas."

Sid took a drag of his smoke. "Cool."

Piper looked toward the row of buildings lining Third Avenue. "Only you would think so, Sid."

He shrugged. "I don't eat vegetables, and besides, I'd do it myself."

I smiled. If Sid ever got a job, and that job had to do with a restaurant, I wouldn't even eat the crackers.

Sid hopped from the wall, digging in his bag and bringing out some beef jerky. As he did, Michael Thorburne walked over to us. Sid nodded to him. " 'Sup."

Michael looked around. "You guys hitting on anything?"

Piper pointed to the other side of the park, a block away. "That side of the park, Mike."

Michael went on. "Got some good stuff if you want. From up north. Strong."

Sid smiled. "We quit. You know that. Everybody does."

He furrowed his brow. "Yeah, sure. Cutter. I didn't know if . . ."

I stood, staring. "Yeah. Cutter."

Michael backed away a step. "Cutter was cool. I'm sorry."

Piper hopped from the ledge, grabbing his board. "I'm clean. Over a year."

Michael nodded. "Didn't mean to mess with you."

"No problem. Just don't ask again," Piper said, uncharacteristically pissed off. He looked at me. "I'm skating the bowl." Then he walked behind the ledge and over to the Monster.

Michael watched Piper leave, then looked at me again. "I didn't mean . . ."

I studied him, wondering why he'd even bring it up. "He's still messed up about it. We all are."

"It was a raw deal."

I shook my head. "Doesn't matter. He's dead. And he's dead because of the shit you sell."

"You know I don't deal the hard stuff, Tate. Just 420. And you know I wasn't involved in the stuff he got ahold of. That was all Lucius and his boys."

Lucius ran all the hard stuff surrounding the school. Meth, crack, scripts, heroin, he did it all, but he was small-time. Two or three guys dealt for him, but he had a monopoly Under the Bridge. I'd seen him several times when he'd come by to check things out. He pretty much kept to himself, didn't talk much, and I liked it that way.

"I know. But don't be stupid, Mike. Stay away from the crew." Just then, I spotted Indy getting out of an old beater station wagon down the street. "Be back in a minute."

Sid flipped his chin toward the vert, his mouth full of jerky. "At the Monster with Pipe. Catch us."

CHAPTER TWO

I dropped my board and skated along the sidewalk, watching as Will opened the driver's door and talked with a guy at the entrance of an old apartment building.

Indy saw me, smiled, and flashed me the peace sign. Angie Simmons, a cross between a Goth chick, white-trash girl, and storage container for STD's, grimaced from the backseat as I came up to them. She defined irritating, and was just barely smart enough to know she was.

Will wore a white wife-beater tank top and faded jeans, with a gold necklace around his neck and several tats running down his shoulders and forearms, including the snake on his neck that slithered down his chest. He was built like an ultimate fighter, and I had to admit the guy was imposing. He studied me, his face a rock, his eyes intense as he hooked his thumbs into his belt loops and leaned against the car.

Indy slapped me five. "Hey, Tater. What's up?"

"Get your report card?"

He grinned. "Naw."

I groaned inside. "Dad's going to be pissed."

He flashed his teeth, blond hair glinting in the sun. "Dad's always pissed."

"Maybe if you went to class, he wouldn't be."

"The only way Dad wouldn't be mad at me is if I was you, and"—he smiled, slugging my shoulder—"I'm not you." He pointed above his head. "See? No halo here."

I shook my head. "Don't start, huh? You know what will happen tonight." Our dad is the kind of guy that you have to know your boundaries with. Indy doesn't know what a boundary is.

Angie smirked, her eyes locked on mine as she called out the window. "What's it like having two mommies, Indy?" She laughed. "You spank him when he does bad, Tater? Wash his mouth out with soap before you put him to bed?"

The best thing to do when around trash is step over it and keep walking, so I ignored her. I turned to Indy. "We're skating the Monster. You coming?"

Will lounged against his station wagon, his voice easy and quiet. "Tater."

I turned to him. "It's Tate."

He nodded. "I heard about you."

I smiled. "Will, right?" I held out my hand. He looked at it for a moment, then shook. I turned back to Indy. "Ready?"

Will's face broke into a grin, his eyes dark, his voice slippery and calm. "So, you're the fighter around here."

The challenge in his voice was there, but I wasn't about to get into a pissing match with a guy I didn't know, so I ignored him. "Pipe and Sid are already there."

Will spoke. "Guess I got the wrong Tater."

I faced him.

He lit a cigarette, still leaning against the car, and exhaled, lifting his chin as the cloud of smoke drifted up. "Problem?"

My chest tightened the way it did before my knuckles ended up bruised. "No."

Will chuckled.

I gritted my teeth, cursing myself for the rage building in me. Other guys could let things go, but I couldn't. Never had, never would, and it irritated me almost as much as this tattooed redneck challenging me. Indy saw it happening, and he flipped his chin at Will. "I'm splitting. Check you later."

Will laughed, and I wondered if the guy was born an asshole or learned it from the Asshole Club of America. "Sure, Indy. No sweat." He looked at me, his eyes flat. "We'll see you later, too, huh?"

Indy sighed as we walked away. "Why do you always do that?"

The tightness didn't fade. "Do what? I just totally let him walk all over me to *not* do that."

He looked at me. "I'm talking about Angie. She's right, you know? You're not Mom."

"Yeah, I know. But you pull this crap and you know what happens. Dad'll rain shit down on you, you'll throw it back on

14

him, he'll get pissed at everybody, and Mom will have to deal with it."

"So? You're not me. And Mom can take care of herself."

"Have you ever thought that living in a war zone all the time gets old? Don't you ever get tired of it?"

He lit a smoke. "No. Dad's a prick. And besides that, you're the one living in a war zone all the time, getting in fights and shit."

I didn't have anything to say about that. I never looked for a fight, and I'd never asked for the reputation in the first place. Some people were good at math. I was good at hitting people.

He laughed. "Don't get me wrong, Tate. Having a brother that can kick ass is cool. But, dude, you're on edge, like, *all* the time now. Like a cork about to pop."

I faced him. "Bullshit, Indy. He was gunning for me, not the other way around. And I backed down because you know him."

"Yeah, and it's killing you right now, isn't it?"

I swallowed. "No. And I'm not on edge."

"Whatever. I saw the look in your eyes."

I shrugged. "The only reason I'm on edge is because Dad is going to blow tonight. You know what he said last time, right? One more time and that was it."

"On his side now?"

"He's our dad, Indy. And he's not that bad. It's like you go out of your way to piss him off."

"He's been pissed at me since the day I was born."

"Well, I'm not running screen for you anymore."

"Never asked you to."

"Things are going to be bad tonight. That's all I'm saying."

He laughed again. "So?"

I clenched my teeth. "So fuck it. I don't want to talk about it anymore."

"You brought it up."

"Well, I'm un-bringing it up."

"Fine."

"Fine."

He slid me a glance, then smiled. "Dork."

"Bigger dork."

He punched my shoulder. "It'll be cool, okay? Now let's skate."

I smiled. There was something about my brother that never let me be mad at him for longer than five minutes. "Sure."

We reached the vert, where Sid was sitting on the edge and Piper carved the walls. We were the only crew there, and after Piper pulled a five-forty on the opposite side, he popped over the edge, slapped Indy five, and sat. "How goes it, Indy?"

"Easy like Weezie."

He grinned. "Had an enjoyable day at school?"

Indy chuckled, unhooking his board from his backpack and digging for his knee pads, which meant one thing. A big trick. "Been working on something during my free time."

Sid took a swig of Red Bull. "Angie doesn't count unless it's on her fingers, and that's only to enumerate how many blood-borne diseases she's had."

Indy smiled. "*Enumerate?* Damn, Sid, you got a fever?"

Sid went on. "*Enumerate* means to count, and no, I have a broken spleen."

"Really? Cool." Indy laughed. "Can you count to nine hundred? Because I've been working on my math."

Piper hooted. "Ah. So that's why you're pulling out the pads. If you can pull a nine hundred off the Monster, I'll tie my balls in a bow and give 'em to you for your birthday, pretty boy."

"I don't like small presents."

Everybody laughed. Piper went on, "Even if you could do a nine hundred, which you can't, the Monster is barely big enough. The pros work their lines on at least twenty-footers, and this ain't a twenty-footer."

There'd been only a handful of guys in the city who could pull a smooth nine hundred, which was hitting the edge of the vert, getting major air, spinning around two and a half times, and landing it without leaving body parts on the ground. Indy pursed his lips. "I'll ride ten bucks that I can do it."

Piper agreed. "Shake."

They shook, and Indy eyed Sid. "How about you, Sid? Up for a little bet?"

"I'd rather wipe my butt with sandpaper."

Indy laughed. "I'll take that as a vote of confidence."

Sid shook his head. "Take it how you want it, but I figure it's hard to collect from a guy with a skateboard implanted in his skull."

Indy stood, tailed his board, grinned like a madman, and

dropped in. He carved back and forth, gaining speed and finding his groove, then pulled a five-forty, spinning and coming down smooth as ice before gaining speed again and launching off the edge. This time he knocked out a seven-twenty, came down wobbly, but held his line.

With a few more warm-up passes and a couple more tricks, half the park was watching as we cheered him on. He was good. Better than me. Better than any amateur sponsored guy in the city. In fact, he'd quit a local sponsor last year because of the politics and all the crap that went into it. He was pure skater, down to the roots.

As Indy rolled back and forth, gaining the speed he needed to pull the nine hundred off, he called out to Piper, laughing like a hyena and telling him to get his money out. Then, as he hit the lip, he twisted, airborne a good four feet up, and spun. Once, twice; then, just as he landed the last half, a little kid, probably about ten years old and padded up like the Michelin Man, puttered along the bottom of the vert, right in Indy's line.

Indy saw the kid and twisted hard just as he landed, sliding the board sideways down the wall and hitting the concrete with a skidding thud. The board spun down toward the kid like a broken helicopter blade, flipping on its side and nailing him on the leg. Michelin Man went down, screaming in pain as they tumbled together.

With Indy lying on the ground stunned from a major shoulder hit and the kid holding his leg and screaming bloody murder, the mother scrambled and half slid down a shallow part of the bowl and ran to them. Pipe, Sid, and I dropped in and went to Indy, who sat up, rubbing his shoulder. His eyes went to the boy as his mother knelt, putting her hands on his shoulders and quieting him down.

Indy's eyes stayed on the kid. "You okay, bro?" he said.

He sniffled, looking at Indy. His mother didn't sniffle. "You should really look where you're going. There are kids around here."

Indy ignored her as we gathered around him. "You okay, little man?" He smiled at the twerp.

The kid nodded. The lady furrowed her brow. She held her son, tucking a strand of hair behind her ear. "You could have broken his leg speeding around like that. It's reckless."

Indy gaped at her. Skating and reckless went together like alcoholics and vodka. Overprotective mommies and skate parks didn't. "Ma'am, I'm sorry, but . . ."

Sid rolled his eyes, his dusty voice sarcastic. "Come on, lady, Pukehead here cut his line big-time, and besides that, he shouldn't be at this end of the park. The shallow bowls are down there." He pointed off toward the other side, where all the kiddies tottered around while their moms sipped coffee and visited with each other.

She set her jaw. "This is a public park, and he can skate anywhere he'd like. And watch your language around my son. He doesn't need to be exposed to your"—she looked at Sid, with his scrappy and skintight jeans, wallet chain hanging from his belt, Anarchy T-shirt, and frayed skate shoes—"kind."

Indy stood, took a step, and squatted in front of the kid.

"Probably a good idea to hang down there, partner. You'll be up for this end in a few years, huh? It can get pretty wild up here." He smiled, tapping the kid's helmet.

The boy nodded, still whimpering and clutching his leg as he leaned into his mother's lap.

Indy stood again, grabbing his board. "You're pretty good on that thing, you know? Just keep practicing and you'll fly, dude. The next Tony Hawk." He looked to the mother. "I'm sorry, ma'am. I didn't mean to hurt him." Then he walked away, rubbing his shoulder. Sid looked at the lady like she was the biggest idiot in the world, and we hit the lip, sitting again and watching her gather her son up.

Pipe shook his head. "I swear to God, when people have kids, they lose all sense of reality. I'm selling mine if I ever knock a girl up."

Sid glowered. "This place sucks now. Mommies coming down acting . . . mommyish. I had a lady yell at me last week for saying *shit*." He shook his head. "Not like I was actually shitting, either. I just said it."

Piper grinned. "Remember in the alley behind O'Doherty's?"

Sid smiled. "Awesome. That was, like, the biggest projectile turd I ever took."

"Dude, you wiped with a piece of cardboard."

"Better than crapping my pants."

I shrugged, wondering why every conversation we ever had evolved into either puke, pee, sex, snot, or crap. "The Monster kicks butt."

Sid grunted. "Just fine with the street, if you ask me. And I'd rather deal with the bangers than yuppies pretending they're better than everybody."

Piper laughed. "At least you always see the bright side of things, Sid."

Sid grumbled, slouching. He glanced over at the lady comforting her kid on the bench. "The only thing bright about me is my white ass in that lady's face. My kind? I'll show her my kind. Check it," he said. Then he stood, unbuckled, dropped trou to the ankles, and bent over, looking at the lady upside down between his knees as his skinny white butt glowed in the shadows Under the Bridge, like a beacon for all pasty and ugly things in the world. "HEY, LADY!" he bellowed, spreading his cheeks. She stared in disbelief, then turned away.

Sid straightened, buckled up, and sat down. No laugh, no smile, just back to business as usual.

Indy reeled, laughing and clapping. "You are the weirdest human being I've ever known."

Sid blew it off, watching the lady get up with her kid and leave. He bared ass all the time, and it always came unexpected. The best ever was when he smashed his butt cheeks against the window of a yoga class downtown and farted. He fogged the window.

Indy smiled, rubbing his shoulder. "I think you scarred her for life."

Sid furrowed his brow. "What? I got a nice ass."

I looked at Indy. "You okay?"

He looked off down the park, toward the lady and her son leaving. "Yeah."

Piper got down to business. "You didn't land it, Indy. Pay up." He held his hand out.

"No way. I had to bail."

He shook his head. "Pay up."

Indy grunted, looking at me. "Borrow ten bucks, Tate?"

I rolled my eyes. "How'd I know."

"Dude, I've been practicing for three weeks. I knew I could do it. Besides, you know Piper doesn't have it, either. We're poor, remember? Poor people don't have money."

I looked at Pipe. "You got ten, Pipe?"

He grinned. "Hell no. We're poor, remember? Poor people don't have money."

I waved them off. "Bet's off, then, you dorks."

Piper busted up. "Waah waah waah. Mr. Lawn Mower Car Washer Guy thinks he's king of the world because he works every once in a while. Ain't you God, Tate."

I shook my head, smiling. Some things never changed.

CHAPTER THREE

After Cutter died, Indy, Piper, and I would hop the bus out to Woodlawn Cemetery once a week, hanging our boards on our packs and walking through the thousands of people not living until we reached Cutter. Sid refused to go, having barely made it through the funeral service without fainting. He'd just stood there with the blood draining from his face, looking like a ghost in a borrowed threadbare suit jacket. I realized that day that people obsessed about the thing they feared the most. Death scared Sid so much he couldn't stop thinking about it.

When we first began visiting Cutter, nobody knew what to do. We'd stand around his grave and stare—each of us into our own thoughts and awkward with the silence. He was dead. Gone. We'd never see him again. I didn't know how to deal with it. Nobody did.

Piper was the one who broke the ice. As we stood around like three idiots, he shook his head, unstrapped his board, and took it to the walkway ten feet away. "Hey, Cutter," he called, "check it." Then he did a backside ollie, the clack of his board echoing in the gloomy silence. Indy smiled, then laughed, and soon enough we were all on the walk pulling tricks for our buddy.

The few visitors spread throughout the cemetery turned their attention to the racket, and within a few minutes, a maintenance man sped up in a golf cart and hopped out. He escorted us to the gates after Piper argued about what respect really was.

Since then, life had taken its course, and as we all moved on with Cutter being gone, we moved in different directions with it. I think Indy and Piper said goodbye to Cutter the day we skated for him, and they'd done it just the way Cutter would have wanted. Of all the places to get kicked out of for skating, a cemetery was probably the worst, and I'm sure Cutter was laughing his ass off from wherever he was.

I still visited him every week, though. For some odd reason, I liked the place. Maybe the peace. The solitude relaxed me, and unlike the others, I guess I still needed that connection. Something more than just memories.

I pulled the cord in the bus to signal my stop, and as the driver braked, I stood, making my way to the door. The gates of Woodlawn sat open, and as I stepped under the shadows of the evergreens and the noise from the bus disappeared, silence overtaking me, the tension in my chest eased.

Cutter liked silence, too. He once told me that his favorite time was just before he went to sleep. Silence. Darkness. Peace. Nobody yelling at him.

Cutter's life had been anything but peaceful, and he'd

lived with his uncle the last year of his life. His mother, Frances, had found another of a string of losers to shack up with, and the guy hadn't wanted a teenager hanging around the house. Cutter came home one day after school and his things were boxed up on the front porch. His uncle Steven took him in.

Most people would probably think that a kid would be shocked by getting kicked out of his own house because his mom's new boyfriend didn't want him there. On the inside, though, that was Cutter's life in a nutshell.

Everybody had excuses for everything, but when you had parents who weren't meant to parent, there was only the truth. Cutter's mom sucked as a human being. Life is rough enough with decent parents, and of all the people I knew, Cutter was the last person to deserve a mother like that.

The cool thing about Cutter was that even though he knew his mom didn't give a shit about him, he was always positive. Almost like he was the adult and she was the child. She'd beat him, we'd see the bruises, and he'd just ask us to have compassion for her. "She's had a rough life," he'd say. We'd tell him to whack her back. Call the cops. Whatever. But he wouldn't. He loved her, and that was that.

Cutter never gave up on it. No matter how many times it would happen, and no matter how many times we'd tell him she was evil spawn, he'd just smile, shake his head, and tell us to give her a break. I couldn't even look at her without wanting to shove my fist down her throat. She was like the bully beating on the kid who wouldn't fight back.

At his headstone, I dropped my pack and sat on the grass.

When I first began visiting by myself, I would just sit, letting the time slip by, thinking about stuff. It was peaceful in a weird way. But after a while, I began talking to him. Almost like he was there.

The breeze whispered.

I sat for a while, picking grass and twisting it between my fingers. I didn't want to go home. Dad would be on the warpath. Indy would be sitting on the couch flipping smart-ass answers left and right, and my mom would be in the kitchen trying to ignore everything while she cooked dinner. Welcome home.

The only time I could ever be late without question was when I came here to visit Cutter. My mom had loved him like one of us, and sometimes I think his death hurt her more than it did anybody. He'd been over at our house so often out of sheer hunger that she'd set the table for him every night, and when she heard he'd died, she changed. The way she looked at Indy and me was different now. Almost like she was afraid.

"War zone at the house tonight," I said in the stillness. "I think it might be a bad one."

I looked at his headstone, wishing it would answer and wishing he hadn't stuck the needle in his arm. *Dude, one time,* he'd said. Just once. We'd all been partying, getting stoned, and Cutter was always the one to push the limits. He was afraid of nothing, and nothing could stop him when he'd decided something.

He'd died on the night of his birthday. I found out later

what had happened that morning to push him so far. I realized too late how much it hurt him. How much she hurt him.

If I'd have known the seriousness of what happened to him earlier that day, the thing that finally pushed him to no limits, I would have literally beat him into a coma to stop him, because he knew what he was doing. He knew what would happen because he made it happen. And me and his mother were the only people who knew. Cutter hadn't died of an accidental heroin overdose. He'd killed himself. I didn't know if he'd done it on purpose, but I knew he did it because he didn't care anymore. I stared at his headstone. "You dumb asshole. You dumb, fucking, selfish asshole."

Silence. An elderly woman visiting a grave four headstones down glanced at me. Her eyes were sad.

I turned my attention back to the grass, twisting the strands together.

"Hello."

I looked up, and the woman stood there. She wore a flowered sundress with a blue sweater. She was old. Really old. The wrinkles in her face were deep. I shook my head. "Sorry."

She chuckled. "The dead might be able to hear, but they can't scold you."

I smiled. "I guess not."

She peered at the headstone. "David Samuel Cutter."

I nodded.

She kept looking at the headstone, noting the dates. "He was young. A brother?"

"Almost." I stopped. "Yeah. He was."

Her voice was soft. "I've seen you visit before. That's very nice."

"I miss him, you know?"

She nodded. "Yes, I know." She paused. "My name is Augustine. Aggy."

"I'm Tate."

Her frail voice floated over the bodies. "Nice to meet you, Tate."

My mother's angry face flashed through me. She'd die of embarrassment if she knew I'd cussed like I had in front of the lady. "I'm sorry for swearing."

A moment passed. She coughed lightly, holding her wispy, thin hand to her mouth. "My husband drank himself to death. I suppose you could say he was a dumb, selfish asshole, too."

I looked at her, surprised that she would swear. "There's a lot of those, huh?"

She smiled. "We all are in one way or another, Tate. It just depends on whose glasses you're looking through."

"Sometimes it's hard to see it that way."

Another moment passed, and she reached down, patting me on the shoulder. "It will get better with time. It always does." Then she walked away, returning to her husband's place in the ground.

I went home.

CHAPTER FOUR

"Why are you late?"

I shut the door behind me. I could hear Mom in the kitchen clattering dishes, getting ready for dinner. I looked at my dad. He stood in the entryway to the hall, his bulk filling the space, boots unlaced, work clothes still on, and a beer in his hand. I set my pack down. "It's Thursday. I was with Cutter."

His face went blank for a moment, and then he nodded. "Did you tell your mother?"

"She knows I go every Thursday," I said, echoing my mom's *Honey, I know he goes every Thursday* coming from the kitchen. She followed up with a hello, and I helloed her back.

He nodded again, taking a swig of his beer and walking across the living room to his recliner. "How was your day?"

"Good." I reached in my back pocket, taking out my grades.

He held his hand out. "Where is your brother?"

"Under the Bridge last time I saw him."

He studied my report card, handing it back to me. "Decent, but you know you could do better. Pick it up, huh?"

"Yessir."

"Go show your mother your grades," he said, looking at the coffee table. "And hand me that remote."

I handed him the remote and walked into the kitchen as Dad flipped on the news. Mom pecked me on the cheek and smiled, taking my grades. "Good. I'll put them on the fridge."

I smiled. "I'm not in sixth grade anymore."

She laughed. "You'll understand one day when you're a mother."

"Ha ha. Funny funny."

She smiled again, stirring the corn as Dad cussed out some reporter for telling him unemployment rose again. "Of course it rose, you stupid asswipe. What do you expect when every bloodsucking company in this country moves to China and pays ten-year-olds to make cheap shit?" Mom kept stirring.

"The school called again today about Indy."

"I figured."

Her voice softened. "I don't know what to do about him. And your father is ready to strangle him."

I shook my head. "I don't know, Mom."

"Why does he do this? I just don't understand."

"I don't know," I said, looking into the living room at my dad. The modern world didn't have room for him, and he didn't have room for it. A cell phone was a waste of money, video games were useless, reality shows and MTV were destroying our youth, and as far as he was concerned, whoever invented the computer should have been aborted. Ask him what an iPod was and he'd guess it was a type of vegetable.

He was the kind of guy who liked life simple, cut-and-dried, and didn't like things getting in the way of that. He worked twelve-hour days as a welder to make ends meet, and he was one of the best in town because he'd done it since he was fourteen. He worked hard, expected us to work hard, and I really didn't blame him for being so harsh. He'd grown up in the mountains of Montana in a cabin twenty-five miles from the nearest highway, he believed in self-reliance, and he lived on respect. If you didn't respect yourself, he didn't like you. At all.

Mom sighed, accepting the fact that tonight wouldn't be a good night. She called out to Dad, "Honey, I'm going to serve Tate now. Would you like your plate, too?"

"You like eating at the table," the reply came in.

"That's okay. I have no idea when Indy will be home, and I'm sure you and he will be talking when he does get here."

The sound went down on the TV, and in a moment, he appeared in the doorway. "I think I'll sit at my table with my family and enjoy the nice dinner you prepared for us. Then I think I'll clear the plates and do the dishes. Just like I do every night," he said, using the tone that said he was on edge.

"Honey . . ."

"Just because our son has no respect for you or anybody else doesn't mean I don't. I won't have this house run by a teenager."

She sighed again. "I just don't want a fight, Dan. Things are bad enough with him without a war."

He growled, "Indy is going to have my boot stuck so far down his throat he won't be able to say a word, let alone fight about it. I told him last time what would happen, and now it's going to happen."

"Dan . . ."

He shook his head. "He's pushed it too far. It stops tonight."

She took the roast from the oven, knowing it was useless. "Meaning that China is going to call and ask you to quiet down?"

He shrugged. "The first day I care about what other people think is the day they put me in the ground."

She turned to him, putting her hand on her hip. "Just like your sons?"

He clenched his teeth, his jaw muscles working. "You know what I mean."

"Yeah, and you know what I mean. We raised them to think and do for themselves and to question authority, Dan, and sometimes we have to pay the consequences for that. He's going through a hard time. Have patience."

The one thing my parents never do is beat around the bush when we're in the room. They're an open book when it comes to family, and it took a while for the crew and all of our friends to get used to it. Since then, I couldn't count how many times Sid or Cutter had wished their parents were so cool.

Unless you cross Dad, that is. Then the world rains shit down on your head.

He finished his beer, crinkling it up and throwing it in the can. We don't recycle because the city gets the money for it without sending him a check, and my dad doesn't believe anything should be free, including saving the earth. "Tate, grab the cups. Three," he said, lifting the stack of four plates from the counter and taking them to the dining room table. He put three of them at their places and brought one back.

Mom's eyes darkened as she watched him put the fourth plate back in the cupboard, but she didn't say anything. I filled the cups with water and set them out. "Anything else, Mom?"

She shook her head. "Dan, will you carve the roast?"

Dad opened the fridge and grabbed another beer. "You said patience, hon. We'll wait until he gets home."

She smacked her spoon down on the stove. "Dan, I don't want this. Not tonight. Please."

He faced her, his voice low and soft. "Steph, I listen to you. I keep my mouth shut when you tell me I should keep my mouth shut. I know when something is important to you and I try, but it's gone too far, and this is between him and me. He knows dinner is ready at seven, he skipped again today, the school is going to take us to court if he continues this, and I goddamn well know he won't have his grades with him," Dad said, looking at me. I avoided his eyes, putting utensils on the table.

She swallowed, picking up the spoon and taking a breath. She stared at the corn simmering. "Please put his plate on the table."

"He's not eating at a table he doesn't respect."

She slammed the spoon down again, splattering corn juice on the stove, and faced him, her eyes blazing. "We already lost one person sitting at our table, Dan, and I won't lose another! Do you understand me?" she said, choking down a sob. She breathed for a moment in the silence of the kitchen, regaining her composure, then went on. "I'm a mother and I feed my children. Set his plate."

A moment passed, the two of them looking at each other, and I could tell a whole conversation was happening in the thin air between them. Dad got a plate and set it out.

I waited in our room, trying to do homework but obsessing about the time. Seven-twenty. Seven-twenty-two. Seven-twenty-five. Seven-thirty. Ten minutes late in my dad's book was enough to get him pissed because late people simply didn't give a crap about other people's time, and I knew a half hour late was on the BALLISTIC section of the chart. Then I heard the door open.

No boom. No explosive bellow. Nothing. I wondered if the nuclear bomb went off so fast I'd died instantly and was in heaven. Then my dad called from the living room that dinner was on. I groaned, heaving myself from my bed.

Mom, Dad, and Indy were sitting at the dining room table when I came out, and as I took my seat, Indy smiled at me. I did a double take, staring at him for a second, then put my napkin on my lap. "Hey."

"Hey."

My dad cleared his throat. "Tate, say the blessing, please?"

I nodded, bowing my head. "Dear Lord, please bless this food. Thanks to Mom for making it, thanks for this house, and if Dad rips Indy's head off and craps down his neck, don't let the blood get in my corn. I'm starving. Amen," I said.

Dad slowly raised his head, his eyes meeting mine and giving me an implicit warning. I smiled, shrugging. "Sorry."

He grunted, adjusting his napkin.

When Indy and Dad weren't at each other's throats, dinner was a cool thing around our house. Sid and Piper joined us often enough, and it was a time when everybody talked and laughed about their day and what was going on. When they fought, dinner was like a silent sanctuary ruled by my mom. Dinner-table law said that if you didn't have anything good to say, shut your trap.

As my dad picked up the tray of beef, he spoke. "How was your day, Indy?"

He rolled his eyes. "Fine."

I looked at him in disbelief, my stomach squirming. I'd seen him like this before. A ton of times, but not in the last year. He was high. I melted inside. This was so wrong on so many levels I couldn't even think about it.

My dad stood and did what he did every night. He walked to my mom's place and dished her main course. Then he sat down and dished his, handing the serving plate to me. "The school called today and said you weren't there, Indy. Was there a mistake?"

Indy sat, waiting for me to finish dishing the roast. "No. I skipped."

"The school is going to take action through the courts if you keep skipping, and you know that. You also know we can't afford it. So, why? Tell me."

Indy's eyes, fogged and red, met his. "Because I'm a loser. You know that, Dad. You tell me all the time."

Dad seethed. "Did you bring your grades home?"

He smiled. "Can't really get them if I'm not there, huh?"

Dad dished his potatoes, and I swear I could actually see a lightning storm brewing above his head. He reminded me of a tornado in a straitjacket, just waiting to burst the seams. "Watch your mouth, son."

He lowered his eyes. "I can't. My eyes won't go down that far."

Dad took a deep breath. A very deep and long breath. Indy was insane, and I was seeing something in him that I hadn't seen before. Something more dangerous than anger or a willingness to fight. He didn't care, and it scared me. After another moment, Dad glanced at Mom, then spoke. "You are high."

Indy sat back, flipping his napkin on the table. "No shit. Who wouldn't be if they had to deal with you every—"

For a man who was built like a tank made of muscle, I had no idea my dad could move so fast. His chair flew behind him as he bolted upright, his thighs hitting the table and spilling all the glasses. A meaty hand jabbed across the table and the next thing I knew, Dad dragged Indy over the table, yanking him to within an inch of his face. Indy's feet dangled a few inches above the floor as dishes scattered. Mashed potatoes smeared his shirt. Mom gasped in shock, and I couldn't believe I was seeing what I was seeing. He'd never touched either of us before.

Dad, with his nose almost touching Indy's cheek, spoke into his ear, his voice a low and vicious growl. "You can screw with me all you want, son, but"—his grizzly voice rose into a bellow—"if you EVER sit at your mother's table again with dope in you, you're out! Got it? You respect her," he said, shaking Indy roughly as he spoke.

Indy smiled. "Go ahead. Do it. I know you want to. Hit me. You're so fucking tough. Do it."

For a moment I thought he would. But he spoke, pointing to Mom, still face-to-face with Indy. "Don't do this to your mother, Indy."

Indy sneered. "Or what?"

Dad reared back his fist, then hesitated, time stopping as he stared at Indy. In that moment, I knew that all the barroom-brawl stories I'd heard about him before he met Mom were true. The rage emanating from him was palpable, and I knew right down to the core of what I was that any human being willing to mess with him was insane.

He didn't hit Indy, though. He shoved him back, off the table. Indy sprawled on the floor, covered in potatoes and flecks of corn. I could see the fear in his eyes, even through the glaze of being stoned. Dad stepped around the table and stood over him. "Apologize to your mother."

Silence. Nobody moved as we waited. Then my mother stood. Her voice shook. "Dan. Enough is enough."

He clenched his teeth. "He's going to apologize or he's going to get more until he does. He knows the rules. Both boys do. He might act like some ghetto street punk, but not in your home."

Mom took a breath, not sure of what to do because our family had just been turned upside down. "Dan, get your keys, get in the truck, and drive around until you're cooled down. Then you'll come home and we'll talk."

Dad stared at Indy, then slowly reached down, grabbed him by fistfuls of his shirt, and pulled him to his feet. He calmly brushed dinner from the front of Indy. His voice, bereft of anger, was slow and smooth. "Apologize to my wife."

Indy looked at me, and something clicked between us. Things had changed. When we were younger and mouthed off to Mom, there'd always been hell to pay, but this was different. We weren't six years old anymore, and I knew right then that when Dad said *Apologize to my wife* instead of *Apologize to your mother,* he wasn't looking at Indy as a child to be disciplined. A final boundary had been crossed, and it scared the crap out of me.

Indy took a breath. "I'm sorry."

Without another word, Dad left. After a minute, Mom nodded and picked up a dish. "Well, let's get this cleaned up, then."

CHAPTER FIVE

"I can't believe you." I sat at my desk, staring at my homework.

Indy was sprawled on his bed, staring at the ceiling. He looked over, turning the volume down on his iPod. "Dad can kiss my ass."

I shook my head. "I'm not talking about that. I'm talking about Cutter."

He shrugged, groaning. "So what? I got high. It's not the end of the world."

"We had a deal."

He rolled his eyes, turning away. "Yeah."

"Why?"

"You knew just like I did what was going to happen when I got home. I just needed to chill."

I grunted. "He was pissed for sure."

He turned back to me, then sat up, running his fingers through his hair. "No, Tate. Not just pissed. You saw it. That was hate, man. He wanted to hit me so bad."

"He doesn't hate you. He just doesn't want . . . He just wants you to do good."

He looked at me. "You know what I wish?"

"What?"

"That I had a fucking cheerleader squad on my side for once. Why do you always defend him?"

"I don't."

"Bull. Yeah, you do."

"Well, he doesn't look for trouble, Indy. You do. Why can't you just lay low for once? Give it a break?"

"Because he never gives me one."

"Yeah, he does."

"Like when? Remember when I asked him to build a half-pipe in the driveway? When we first got into skating?"

I nodded. "Yes. And he built it."

"No, dude, he didn't. He said we didn't have the money, until you wanted one also—then we suddenly had the money. Same with everything else. You get an F on a test and he tells you to pick it up. Just try harder next time, right? I get an F and he goes off the deep end, telling me I'm wasting everything." He paused, looking at the floor, then lay back down. "Whatever. I'm done talking."

"You know why he does it, Indy."

"Enlighten me."

"Because you're smart and I'm not. And he knows it. You're, like, the most brilliant idiot in the world and everything could be easy for you. I have to study and work to do

41

anything good, and you don't. You could pass every class you have without cracking a book open, but you won't. So he rides you."

"Great. Makes me feel so much better."

"You know what I'm saying."

"I know. And I didn't ask for it. School isn't for me, and as far as Dad is concerned, I've never been for him. You like wrenching on the truck with him and fixing stuff and watching sports and fishing. All that crap."

I shrugged. "You don't like those things."

"No shit. But why can't he like anything I do?" He pointed at his computer. "When was the last time he read one of my stories? Huh?"

I clenched my teeth, frustrated. It was funny, because while Indy hated school and everything about it, he wrote stories constantly. And they were good. But Dad didn't like them because Indy wrote about life. Real life. And that included sex, drugs, and cusswords. Things that Dad thought were ruining our country. "I don't know."

"I do. I don't fit into his stupid redneck world because if you don't like football or trucks or shooting shit with guns, you're not good enough for him."

"He doesn't see things that way, and you know it."

"Whatever."

A few moments passed. I knew it was useless to talk anymore, because every time we did, he just got so worked up that he exploded. "Just don't get high again, okay?"

He closed his eyes. "Sure."

"Promise."

"I promise," he said, then opened an eye, peering over at me. "Dork."

I smiled. "Bigger dork."

CHAPTER SIX

Gunmetal clouds blanketed the sky, and a few claps of thunder rumbled through the neighborhood, threatening to bring rain. Dad hadn't said a word that morning to Indy, and they avoided each other until we left for Under the Bridge. There was a silence in the house that I couldn't really describe, other than being reminded of a funeral home, and I was glad to get out.

As we hit the curb in front of the house and dropped our boards to head out, Dad came out of the garage and called to Indy. I stayed at the curb for a couple of minutes while they talked, and when Indy came back, his face could have been cut from stone. I sighed. "What's up?"

"Dad bought a home drug-testing kit at the store last night. I'm also grounded to the house every day after school to do homework, which he'll check. And if I skip again, Mom will drive me to school every day and pick me up, and I can't leave the house at all for the rest of the year, including summer."

"Wow. Hard-core. Did you tell him you weren't going to smoke anymore?"

"No. Why would I?"

I rolled my eyes as we began walking. "Well, because you're not going to."

He shrugged. "He has the drug test for that, and besides, I guess I'm a liar now, too."

"Did he say you were a liar?"

"Tate, why would he get a fricking drug test if he thought I'd be honest about it? I've never lied, man. Every time they've asked, I've told them."

"What are you going to do?"

He laughed. "Well, if I'm a liar now, I guess I'll live up to his expectations."

"Dude, don't."

"Why not? I've got nothing to lose."

"Only your freedom. You want to be stuck in the house for the rest of the year?"

He dropped his board, the clatter echoing down the street as he hopped on it. "Ain't gonna happen, bro. Come on, the crew is there already."

• • •

The park was crowded when we arrived, and as we sat back watching some guys trying to tackle the Monster, Indy relayed to Sid and Piper "last evening's entertainment." I was surprised that he left out the part about getting high, but I didn't say anything about it.

Piper munched on a bag of Doritos, stuffing chips in his mouth. "Let's hit the six set at the church, huh? Too busy here."

Sid stood. "I'm out. My aunt Carol called this morning and offered me twenty bucks to do yard work."

Piper laughed. "You? Work? What's wrong with that picture?"

Sid grabbed his board. "My dad blew all our money gambling again, and I need lunch money for next week."

We bumped fists. "Cool. See you later."

Sid left, and as the clock on the church tower reached four o'clock and the bells sounded, we skated across the empty parking lot. When we rounded the corner, a few junior high kids were skating the set of stairs. Piper spit. "Grom action."

Groms were different than the kidlets skating the park with their pads and helmets and their moms clapping every time they pulled a manual for longer than two seconds. Groms were younger street skaters. With dirty clothes, long hair, worn-out sneakers, and street attitude, groms skated the city looking for good stuff to roll on. They were us a few years ago.

I nodded as we neared. "Cool. One of 'em is Mitchell." Mitchell was a seventh grader at Sacajawea Middle School, and the kid and his crew lived on their boards. I saw him everywhere, and I mean everywhere. Sometimes I wondered if he ever went home.

Mitch saw us and waved, threw an ollie down the six set like it was nothing, and skated toward us. Brown dirty hair down over his collarbone, bangs in his eyes, a small nose, and big ears made him look almost like a mouse. He smiled, show-ing a gap in his teeth. He'd taken a fall last year, trying to ride a grind rail at the Bank of America on Riverside Avenue, and knocked a tooth out. "Hey, Tater. What's up?"

"Park's busy."

He laughed. "Park sucks now. I like ghetto fabulous better."

Indy and Piper skated off to the far side of the parking lot, piling two concrete parking dividers on top of each other to kick-flip over. I looked at Mitchell's board. "New deck, huh?"

He beamed. "Yeah. Saved for two weeks raking lawns, and my dad said he might get me some trucks in a while." He turned his board over, showing me. "Axle thread is stripped. Wobbles, you know?"

The last time his dad put out any dough for Mitchell was paying the hospital for his birth. I nodded. "I've got an extra pair sitting around until then if you want them."

He brightened. "How much?"

I shook it off. "Nothing. I got new ones and the old ones are just sitting there. Come on over in the next couple of days and we'll bolt 'em on. We'll work your bearings over, too."

He smiled. "Awesome." He set his board down and skated to his buddies at the stairs. Piper and Indy had three dividers stacked up now. Indy cleared it, but Pipe took a digger, his board clattering as he hit the pavement. I laughed as I skated over to them. "Kick it higher, Pipe."

He got up, rubbing his palms. "Yeah, sure. I don't have springs in my feet, man."

Indy hit it again, pulled a one-eighty with the kick, and landed it, wobbling a bit but keeping his balance.

Piper spit again. "You suck, Indy."

Indy laughed. "Your sister sucks."

"Ha ha, asswipe. If I had a sister, she wouldn't be into losers like you." His eyes twinkled. "Go back to your sponsor if you're so good, weenie boy."

Indy raised his chin, showing Piper his neck. "See this, man? No leash attached." Indy had been offered a sponsorship by a local board shop and he'd taken it, but after a while, the politics and crap of selling out got to him, and he quit.

Piper's eyes went across the parking lot to Mitchell and his friends. "Speak of the devil."

We turned, and four skaters—including Corey Norton, who had two local sponsors and was gunning for a national board-company sponsorship—skated around the corner toward Mitchell and his buddies. Corey had taken Indy's place when he bagged on the sponsorship, and there was definite bad blood between his crew and ours. Corey thought he won the sponsorship over Indy. Not the case. And besides that, Corey was a rich prick.

We watched for a minute as Corey and his crew skated the stairs, shouldering the kids out of the way and moving into their spot. Mitch, who reminded me of a firecracker on wheels, kept skating, holding his ground.

Piper saw me staring. "He can handle himself, Tate. Don't sweat it."

I shook my head. "Twelve-year-olds against seventeen-

48

year-olds. That guy is a jerk." I watched as Corey rode across Mitchell's line as he jumped the set of stairs, blocking his landing. Mitchell dodged midair to miss and tumbled down the last two steps, his board flying and landing at Corey's feet. It bounced and hit Corey's board.

Corey yelled at him, and Mitchell, on his butt and rubbing his skinned elbow, gave him the finger and yelled something back. Corey, his face twisted and pissed off, bent down, picked up Mitch's new deck, and slammed it down against the stair rail, snapping it in half and throwing it down.

I set my board down and skated, with Piper and Indy following. Halfway there, I flipped my board up and walked. Piper and Indy joined me. Piper snorted. "Uncool, man. That was way uncool."

I didn't say anything, just walked, my eyes on Corey.

Indy bumped my arm. "Tate . . ."

I ignored him. As we neared, all heads turned. Mitch was on his feet and picking up his busted board. I faced Corey. "What's your problem?"

Corey stared at me. "He got in my line."

I faced Corey, then looked at Mitch. Blood ran down his elbow. "You okay, Mitch?"

He nodded, half of his broken board in his hand and a crushed expression on his face. Unless he stole to get a new one, he'd be walking for weeks. I knew chances were he'd steal.

I stared at Corey. "Give me your wallet."

Corey smirked. "This isn't your deal, Tate."

Piper set his board down, standing beside me. "Why'd you do that, man?"

Indy shook his head. "I knew you were low, Corey, but that was really low."

Corey grimaced at Indy. "Maybe if you put as much time into your board work as you do your mouth, you'd be able to find a sponsor, Indy."

Indy smiled. "I'm not a sellout, and besides, I could hammer you any time of the day."

Corey smirked again. "You and me and the vert, man. I'll walk all over you, same as I did to get your spot on the team." He paused, then grinned. "Better yet, why don't you and your crew beg for a sponsor and go up against us at the Invitational? We'll be there."

I cut in. "Hand it over, Corey."

Corey's face twisted into a sneer. "What, you're going to rob me?"

Corey's crew laughed, all but a guy named Stick. Even though he was on the same team, I never knew why he hung with Corey. He was cool. I glanced over at Mitch, and then I swung. My knuckles throbbed, and the jolt of the impact against Corey's cheek cracked up my arm and into my shoulder as he flew back, twisting away and down to the pavement.

Blood flowed from his nose as he rose, and I rushed him, spinning him around and putting him in a headlock. Three quick rights into his ribs later, I yanked him around, grabbing a handful of hair and pulling him straight. "Give me your wallet."

Blood streaked down his shirt, his breathing was ragged,

and as I looked in his eyes, I saw fear. He dug in his back pocket, taking his wallet out. I took it with my free hand and threw it to Indy, then brought Corey close, talking low. "You mess with him again and I'll trash you." Then I shoved him back.

He skidded on his butt, bracing himself with his arms and gaping at me. "You're a psycho, man. Total psycho." He looked at his crew. "Dude's a psycho."

I studied him for a moment. "Call the police, Corey. See what happens."

Silence. He fidgeted. His crew waited. I noticed a family getting out of a sweet-looking Lexus in the parking lot. A man, a woman, and two girls. They stared at the scene, and the lady flipped open her phone, dialing.

One of the girls was my age, and I recognized her from English. Kimberly Lawson. Varsity cheerleader and volleyball player. She was an inch taller than me, and I'm six feet. Superstar girl.

Indy hooted, looking through Corey's wallet. He took a condom out and held it up. "You hold these for your mom, Corey?" Then he laughed, flicking it at him.

I shook my head, looking at Corey's ruined face, and I almost got sick. "Knock it off, Indy."

Indy rolled his eyes, then dug in the wallet again. "There's eighty bucks in here."

I glanced at Mitch. "How much was the deck?"

Mitch sniffed, his eyes wide as he stared at me. "Thirty-two bucks at Badger's."

I nodded. "Take forty, Indy."

Indy took two twenties and folded the wallet up. He threw it to Corey.

I looked at Corey. "Get out of here."

They did, with Corey wiping his bloody nose on his stained shirt as they went. Mitch stood back, away from us. I took the twenties from Indy, glancing at Kimberly as they went in a side door to the church. "Come on, Mitch."

"Where?"

"Badger's."

He smiled, beaming. "Right now?"

I steamed. "Yeah. Right now."

Indy shook his head. "Tater the superguy."

I glowered. "Shut up, Indy. Your mouth is going to get you nailed one of these days. You know that, right?"

"Me, nailed? I tried to warn the guy. And let's see, I haven't been in a fight in . . . never. Let's see about you, though." He counted off on his fingers. "That guy down at McDonald's last year, Paul Tyson in the parking lot this spring, Kyle Jefferson in the courtyard, two guys at the park who you literally creamed, that Indian dude who tried to steal your wallet, and now Corey. And that doesn't count junior high. I don't have enough fingers for that."

Piper smiled. "The only reason you never have to fight is because everybody in this city knows your brother. You have an impenetrable shield of Tate armor around you."

Indy screwed his eyes up. "Whatever. I'm bagging off anyway. Meeting somebody."

Piper hit Indy's shoulder. "What's her name?"

Indy flashed a grin. "Wouldn't you like to know."

I watched as Indy skated away, then turned to Mitch. "Ready?"

"Yeah."

Piper looked at me.

"What?" I said.

"That *was* pretty hard-core, Tate."

I shrugged. "You saw what he did."

"Yeah, but . . ."

I turned to him. "But what? He broke the board, he pays for it. Besides, I asked him three times, and it's not like Mitch could have clocked him."

"Sure, Tate, I'm just saying . . ."

I looked at Piper. "You were saying you were going to buy him a new board? Is that it? Because otherwise, I don't see a solution."

Piper didn't answer.

I nodded. "Leave it alone, then, huh? Things are shitty, and I don't want them shittier. Besides, the cops are going to roll up in a minute. That lady called."

Piper nodded, dropping the subject as the three of us walked toward Badger's skate shop. A moment passed. "So, have you thought about the Invitational?" he said.

The Pro Skater Invitational was coming to the Spokane Veterans Arena in a little under three weeks. Huge pipe, a circuit of pro skaters, and major TV coverage. The deal with this skate tour was that in every city they went to, any local sponsored amateur could compete with other local amateurs the day before the event. The winner in each city would get a national sponsorship. And it would be televised, which was a huge opportunity for national exposure.

"We're not sponsored."

"I know, but have you thought about it?" Piper asked.

"We're street skaters, and corporate sucks, remember?"

Piper eyed me. "You can tell me that all you want, Tate, but I know you want to go sponsored. I've known it since last year. Since Indy bailed on it."

I shrugged, happier with his not-serious side.

He went on. "Just because Sid and Indy hate the corporate gig doesn't mean you have to. Or me."

I furrowed my brow. "You've thought about it?"

He looked around, like he was making sure nobody could hear the sinful words coming from his mouth. "Sure. It would be sort of cool, you know? Pros make bucks, too." He shrugged. "We'd have a chance to get noticed, man. And I don't know about you, but I don't want to spend the rest of my life making ten bucks an hour doing shit I don't want to do."

"I haven't thought about it." Even as I said it, I knew it wasn't true. I had thought about it. A lot. The spoken and unspoken code with the crew was that selling out to the sponsors was as bad as being a politician. But that didn't make imagining being on top of that pipe, with all those people watching, any less real.

"No sweat. See ya tomorrow, huh? Under the Bridge?"

"Yeah, sure."

. . .

Bill Badger owned the Hole in the Wall, on a red-bricked side
street in the downtown core, just a few blocks away from the
church. Half of his shop held boards and wheels and trucks
and just about anything else you would need for skating besides helmets, pads, and any other protective gear. The other
half held punker hair dye and racks of earrings, gauges, bongs,
incense, and various other counterculture merchandise.

Mitch and I walked in, and Badger sat behind the counter
on his stool as usual, popping Tootsie Rolls into his mouth
from the huge jar next to the cash register. Badger was a
throwback to the heavy-metal eighties. Not even a throwback, really. In the fog of dope surrounding his big head over
the last twenty or so years, he'd been caught in a vortex of
time.

Probably around thirty-five years old, he once told me he
woke up and noticed the century mark had passed, then went
back to sleep when he didn't like what he saw. Badger weighed
in at a good 260 pounds, had long, scraggly brown rocker hair,
and thought clean clothes were a waste of water. A truly odd
recipe of lazy, environmental, hard-core, and hippy made
Badger one-of-a-kind.

This week he wore a Black Sabbath shirt with a huge
mustard stain on it, and old-school metal blasted through
the stereo system in the small place. We walked past the
bongs, incense holders, punker hair dye, and rocker posters

and up to the counter, where the skate stuff was. He grabbed the remote and turned the music down, tossing a Tootsie Roll to Mitch. "Today is Sabbath day. Name a song by the renowned band Black Sabbath and you may shop in here."

I smiled. "Hey, Badge."

He raised his eyebrows. "Name a song or I'm calling the pigs."

"Um, 'Livin' After Midnight,'" I said.

He slumped, pointing to the speakers, which apparently held the answer to the question. "You disgrace the hallowed band Sabbath, dude. 'Living After Midnight,' my young sinner, is from another and very respectable band called Judas Priest, which I must say is talented, but not of the Sabbath level."

Mitch spoke up. "'Iron Man.'"

Badge grinned. "At least there's one young soul educated in the historical wonders of where the trash you listen to now comes from. You may both stay in my store."

"We're here to get a new deck."

Mitch put both ends of his busted board on the counter.

Badger studied it. "You just bought this here. What's up?"

Mitch stuffed his hands in his pockets, grinning. "Some guy snapped it. Tate beat him up, though."

Badger shook his head. "Violence is never the way, Tate. Gandhi once said to turn the other cheek."

"Jesus."

He looked at me. "You called?"

"Jesus said that. Gandhi laid down in front of soldiers or something."

He shrugged. "They both wore white robe things. Same difference."

I laughed. "Sure, man."

Badger picked up an end of the board and studied it. "Do I know the person who did this?"

"No. Sponsored guy from the Wheelhouse," I said.

"Corey Norton." Mitch spoke up.

"Aaah. My competitor and the leader of their team. I rescind my previous statement and now condone violence. Only against competitors' customers, though." He stood from his stool. "Be right back."

Mitch and I stood at the counter while Badger grabbed an identical deck from the rack, bringing it over. He looked at Mitch in his torn T-shirt and holes-in-the-knees Levi's. "On the house, kid. You come by after school and stock shelves for a couple of days and we have a deal."

I shook my head. "He has money, Badge."

Mitch smiled. "He took it from Corey. To pay for it. You shoulda seen the sucker's face, Badge." Mitch made a face mimicking a horror-flick monster. "All busted up. Bam!"

Badge nodded, pondering as he looked at me. "I see. Violence and strong-arm robbery. You're moving up the ladder."

I shrugged.

Badger dug under the counter, bringing out a screwdriver and socket set. "We'll get you set up, huh? Grip tape, buff the rails, a tweak here and there, and you're set."

Mitch smiled again and watched as Badger worked. I dug in my pocket. "How much was it?"

"Thirty-two bucks. No tax if you've got cash."

I put the two twenties on the counter and he opened the till, handing me eight back. I stuffed it in my pocket. "Listen, I've got to split. Thanks, Badge." I hit Mitch on the shoulder. "Stop by sometime and we'll get you set up on those trucks, huh?"

Mitch smiled, staring at his new board. "Yeah, sure. Thanks, Tate."

"No problem. Take it easy, and let me know if that guy looks sideways at you, okay?"

He nodded, and I went home.

CHAPTER SEVEN

Monday rolled around, and so did Indy. Under the threat of being shackled to a post in the basement for the next year, Indy went to school, but of course nothing could be so simple in my brother's life.

My third-period class is on the upper floor of the school, and Indy's is seven doors down. When he did decide to go to school, we'd usually meet at our lockers and grab our stuff for lunch. As I made my way through the mass of people filling the hall, I spotted Indy at his locker. I smiled when I reached him. "Crazy."

He stowed his backpack on the hook. "What?"

"You being here after three hours."

He took his board out, laughing. "Yeah. Doing nothing all morning has given me time to think about things."

I narrowed my eyes, looking at him. "I'd like to think when a person says that, it means good things."

He turned to me. "Depends on what *good* means and who it's good for."

I grunted. "Shit."

"Look at it this way. The school is going to use that Becca Law if I skip, which will make Mom and Dad go to court and cost them money, and Dad will miss his treasured work if I do, right? He might even have to drag me across the table again."

"Yeah," I said. If a kid skipped too much, the school could send the parents to court over it, and the parents could be fined if the kid didn't start going to school. Indy was ripe for it.

"So, I don't want to go to school."

"So? You're here."

He shook his head. "No. You're not getting it, bro. The only way I can not be here and not go to court is if they don't let me be here. Everybody wins, and Dad can't do a thing because he told me not to skip. He didn't say crap about being suspended."

I clenched my teeth. "Indy . . ."

He set his board down. "Check it," he said, then took off, skating down the hall, bumping past people, carving a path back and forth. People hugged lockers and cheered as he threw kick-flips and ollies, the clack of his wheels echoing through the place.

Even though my stomach churned when I thought about what would happen later, I couldn't help but envy him. He had no fear. No boundaries. Skating was about freedom and about breaking rules for a reason, and there was something inside my brother that lived for it. He did stupid things, but he never did them for stupid reasons. Regardless of the consequences. This was for my dad, and no matter how I felt about it, I understood where he was coming from.

As he hit the end of the hall, turned around, and began skating back, a few teachers came out of their classrooms, wondering what the issue was. That included Mr. Halvorson, the baseball coach and head of the English department. He saw Indy rolling toward him and lunged, grabbing him by his shirt and yanking him up against a row of lockers. Indy's board rolled on. I picked it up, walking toward them.

By the look on Mr. Halvorson's face and the way the tendons in his neck stood out as he growled at Indy, I knew things were going to get out of hand. Halvorson was a big guy with a reputation for being the ultimate jock, and he looked like he was about to make Indy a part of the locker. I double-timed it, getting there just in time to hear Indy ask him where he hid the steroid needle marks. Halvorson's grip tightened on Indy's shirt. "This school has just about had enough of you, young man."

Indy smiled. "You know what? We see things the same. You don't give a shit if I exist, and I don't give a shit if you get hit by a truck tomorrow. Even, huh?"

I broke in. "Knock it off, Indy."

He looked at me, still pinned to the locker. "Awesome. It's my brother. You want to join in, Tate? Maybe take turns telling me how much this school wants me around? At least this jackhole is honest about it."

Mr. Halvorson loosened his grip on Indy, and I saw

something in his expression change. "I'll escort you to the office." He looked at me. "You can go on to class."

. . .

By fifth period I knew Mom had been to the office and Indy was back at the house, and for the first time throughout all the petty and stupid arguing between my dad and my brother, I didn't want to go home. For the first time, I suppose, I knew something had snapped for both of them. We'd always been a family, and now that wasn't the case.

Things were going from bad to worse faster than I could count, and I didn't know where it would end up. My dad was not a man to cross, Indy was born to cross him, and neither would stop. They were poison to each other, and I couldn't be the remedy. Nobody could.

On the way to sixth period, I spotted Corey Norton at his locker, sporting two black eyes and a swollen nose. I tapped him on the shoulder, and he flinched when he turned and saw me. We stood there for a moment, and I studied his face. Not bad for one punch. He frowned. "You broke my nose." It came out nasally.

I dug in my pocket, taking out the eight dollars left over from the deck. I held it out to him. I wasn't too interested in feeling sorry for a guy who would do that to a kid. "Leave him alone."

He looked at my outstretched hand, then took the money. "I could press charges, you know."

I turned around and walked away. He wouldn't. He couldn't. His entire credibility in this school as a skater would vanish if he did. He'd lick his wounds and avoid me, or he and his buddies would find me alone somewhere and beat the hell out of me, but I didn't care either way. I'd been busted up a few times and could handle once more. Corey was a coward and a bully, and nothing would change that.

The girl I'd seen in the church parking lot, Kimberly Lawson, sat three seats ahead of me in sixth-period English. When I walked into class, she was sitting at her desk as usual, on time, on the ball, and with her hair pulled back in a ponytail. I'd never seen her late, never seen her look bored or disinterested during the hour-long monologues Mr. Cassidy gave every day, and never seen her without her hair in a ponytail.

Kimberly Lawson was every daddy's dream come true. Pretty, smart, responsible, talented, a rule follower, and completely and utterly difficult to get close to, which I thought was funny. I'd seen half the football and baseball teams crash and burn with her since junior high, but they still kept trying. Like lemmings flocking over the cliff's edge, they just mindlessly kept heading toward that fateful death drop.

Word was Kimberly Lawson was a lesbian, but it was a quiet word, just like Kimberly Lawson was a quiet girl. Guys could be bitter when repeated attempts to get laid didn't work out. Being a girl in high school, I thought, would suck. If you put out, you were a slut, and if you didn't, you were gay. She'd had two short-lived boyfriends in the past three years that I knew of, but I hadn't known either guy. Kimberly Lawson, besides being the best volleyball player in the school's history, was a mystery if you wanted to know her and just another invisible student walking the halls if you didn't. I'd never wanted to know her, even if she was pretty. Not my type.

She stared at me as I walked past her and sat down, her big brown doe eyes neither afraid nor questioning. Just there, like she was. Two moving eyeballs stuck in a face painting. Mr. Cassidy began his lecture for the day, this one beginning a section on writing essays. I stared at him, not hearing a word he said as I thought about Kimberly. She probably thought I was some kind of criminal or street thug, and for some reason, it bothered me.

Fifty minutes later, class let out and I followed Kimberly to the hall. "Hey." She kept walking, her long legs outpacing mine. I hustled up behind her, tapping her on the shoulder. "Hey."

She stopped, turning. Her eyes sharpened. "Yes?"

"I saw you. At the church."

She didn't smile, didn't say anything, just stared at me.

I cleared my throat. "That was your family?"

She nodded, her eyes flicking away.

I took a breath. Talking to this chick was like pulling teeth. "It's not what it looked like." I don't know why I said it, and I don't know why I cared, but I did.

"You mean beating up Corey and taking his money?"

"Yeah. I mean, no. It wasn't that."

"You didn't beat him up and take his money?"

I looked at her. "Yeah, I did. But not for a bad reason."

She smirked. "I didn't know there was a good reason for beating people up and stealing."

I looked at her and knew it was useless. I knew what she saw when she looked at me. "I just . . . Never mind. You wouldn't get it." Then I walked away.

I contemplated skating until dinner, but something in me pointed my board home. I chuckled as I went, reminded that my mom had once told me that people are sometimes drawn to what hurts them more than what's good for them. For all I knew, the walls would be splattered with battle blood and I'd find Indy's head hanging on a stake in the front yard, but I had to know.

CHAPTER EIGHT

I got home at three and the house was silent. Mom's car was gone, and when I walked inside, the blinds were pulled shut and Dad sat in his recliner, staring at the dead TV. A bad, bad sign, because it meant he was brooding. He held a bottle of beer in his hand, and three more empties made a row on the table beside him. My dad was not a heavy drinker, and certainly not in the middle of the day. He wasn't at work, either. "Hey, Dad."

"Hello." He didn't turn his head, just stared at the blank screen.

I decided playing dumb was the best thing, even though I'd never seen my dad drink four beers before three in the afternoon. "Cut loose from work early, huh?"

"Yes."

"You okay?" I said.

"Yes."

"Indy around?"

"No."

"Out skating?" I looked around. Then I saw it. Indy's board. Snapped in half and lying on the carpet. The war had already been waged. "Holy shit," I blurted out. "What happened?"

"Watch your mouth," he growled.

I took a breath. "Yessir. Sorry."

A moment passed, and he cleared his throat. "Your brother is not living here anymore."

Silence. I couldn't think of anything to say.

"We decided it would be in his best interests if he left."

"Where'd he go?"

"That's not my concern. He chose not to abide by my rules, and he'll pay the consequences."

"Where's Mom?"

"Out."

I sighed. "She's pissed at you?"

He swiveled his head to me. "Not your business, Tate."

"God, Dad, what happened?"

He furrowed his brow, his thick neck flushed from the booze and his eyes fierce. "Let it go if you're smart."

The tone in his voice told me everything I needed to know. "Sure. You need anything?"

"Another beer."

I went to the fridge and grabbed a beer for him, not wanting to, but not wanting to have my head ripped from my neck, either. I handed it to him.

Silence.

I grabbed my board, heading toward the door. I turned back, looking at him. "Hey, Dad?"

He didn't look at me. "Yes?"

"I'm sorry."

He slowly nodded. "So am I, son."

I left then, heading out to find Indy. The first place I went was Under the Bridge, but he wasn't there, so I headed to the Hole in the Wall, where Badger sat behind his counter eating Tootsie Rolls. He popped one in his mouth. "He said you'd come skulking around here."

"Where is he?"

He shrugged. "Don't know. He said if he told me, he'd have to have you kill me."

"Come on, Badge."

"Totally serious. He came in, asked if he could stay in the back; I told him I wasn't running a youth hostel and that it might look like I was boffing a teenager; he bought a new board and then left. But he made me promise on the rocker oath that I wouldn't tell."

"A new board?"

"Yeah. Nicest one I've built in a long time. Birdhouse trucks, fine deck, the whole shot. He paid my Visa bill this month."

I shook my head. I knew he didn't have money for it. At least honest money. "Who was he with?"

"Nobody."

My mind reeled through everybody he knew. Piper and Sid would be a decent bet, but he'd know I'd come looking.

Maybe that guy Will. My heart sank at the thought of that. Then there was Porkchop, a guy he knew well enough but who I'd never met. Before he quit smoking, Indy got his stuff from him. I didn't know exactly where he lived, though. "You know a guy named Will?"

"No. Never heard of him."

"What about Porkchop?"

He nodded. "Porkchop Jones. Went to school with him back when, and he gets me my smoke. Dope dealer."

"Where does he live."

He shook his head. "I don't answer questions that get me involved in family issues, dude. Sorry. I'm like Sweden and Guatemala. Neutral."

I stared at him. "It wasn't a question."

He held his hands up. "Whoa. No need to beat the crap out of me. I'm just a fat dude eating candy, man. Calm down."

"He's my brother, Badger. Tell me."

He looked at me and knew I was serious. "Cascade Creek Trailer Park. Taylor Avenue. Space twenty-seven. And if you don't mind me elaborating a tad bit, I would offer that you might have a slight issue with visiting violence on people for reasons not usually condoned as worthy. That and killing small animals sometimes precipitate becoming a serial killer. Does your mother know you are a pre–serial killer?"

"Thanks."

"You didn't hear it from me, man. Just don't sneak in my room one night and jab my eyeballs out with an ice pick."

"No sweat." I turned to the door.

"Hey, Tate?" Badger called.

"Yeah?"

"Porkchop is . . . odd."

I looked at him for a moment, then nodded. I'd start with Porkchop, because I knew that Indy, after what had happened at home, would be looking for weed. "Thanks."

CHAPTER NINE

Peeled paint and a crooked sign reading CASCADE CREEK TRAILER PARK let me know I had the right place, and from the look of the trailers as I skated down the lane, a dealer named Porkchop would fit right in. This wasn't Grandma and Grandpa's peaceful retirement community where they bought their double-wide and strolled down to the community center for a good game of rummy. This was the back hills of Alabama on crack.

I counted three pit bulls and two Rottweilers chained outside rickety trailers by the time I found the slot, and I stood in the road for a minute studying the place. Three bald tires lay stacked next to a chewed-up garden hose; rust-colored water stains streamed down the sides of the dirty white trailer where the rain gutters were broken; three fifty-five-gallon oil drums filled with broken appliances, car parts, trash, and beer cans stood sentry in front of a broken-down shed at the rear of the parking place; and an old Ford Escort with a coat hanger stuck in the antenna hole sat on the gravel parking pad, like a half-dead dog with open sores covering its hide.

I walked up the way and knocked on the door. Nobody answered, so I knocked again.

"Who's there?" The yell came from inside, muffled, frenetic, high-pitched, and irritated.

I knocked harder, and a second later, the window curtain next to the door flashed open and I saw half a gaunt and hard-living face peek out. The door flew open, and a guy in his early thirties, dressed in dirty jeans and a ripped flannel shirt and with long straggly hair, craned his neck out at me. His eyes bulged from his ruddy face. "You got the wrong place, buddy." Then the door slammed shut.

I knocked again. The door flew open, and the guy craned his neck at me again, his tendons straining. "I don't buy Avon, don't know how to read, don't wear cologne, don't want no insurance, and sure as hell ain't going to buy nothing from you, so you might as well just turn your ass around and go knockin' somewhere else."

I looked him up and down, noticing the butt of a pistol stuck in his waistband. "Are you Porkchop?"

He narrowed his eyes at me. One of the bloodshot orbs wandered just a little bit. He jutted his chin out. "What are you staring at?"

I looked at his regular eye. "I'm looking for my brother. Indy."

He narrowed his eyes even more, barely slits. "You a cop?"

There is nothing more dangerous in this world than a

really dumb guy with a gun, and I wasn't about to get shot. "Is he here?"

He looked over his shoulder. "Hey, Indy, there's a guy out here says he's your brother, but he looks like a cop. You here?"

Indy came to the door. His eyes were glazed. "Hey, bro."

Porkchop smiled at me. "Hell, boy, you shoulda told me you was his brother. Come on in. We can get high." He stepped back, opening a space for me.

I stayed on the porch. "Come home, Indy."

He was so high he was floating. "I'm fine right here, Taterbaby."

I looked at Porkchop, then glanced at the pistol again. "Would you mind giving us a minute, sir?"

He nodded, gesticulating wildly. "Shit yeah, man. I got me some Spam cookin' anyway. Nothin' worse than burning your damn Spam, huh?" Then he disappeared into the trailer, cackling about burned Spam.

I looked at Indy. His lip was swollen. "Did Dad do that?"

He smirked. "Yeah. He broke my board, so I shoved him. Did you know Dad doesn't like being shoved?"

I knew Dad hadn't hit him with a closed fist. If he had, Indy's head would have been half caved in. "Pretty bad situation?"

He smiled. "He's tired of Indy not being like Tate."

I ignored it. "Are you suspended?"

He nodded. "Doesn't matter. I'm not going back."

"Come home."

"Dad kicked me out until I learn how to be a good little boy."

"He said you left."

He shrugged.

"You're staying here?"

He laughed. "It's actually quite palatial. Would you like to join us for dinner? Spam. I think the wine selection this evening is Mad Dog 20/20. Fine by any dining standard."

"If I talk to Dad, will you come home?"

"No."

"Why?"

"Because he's an asshole."

"Indy . . ."

"Hey, man, I went to school. I did what he said."

I clenched my teeth. "Now who's being the asshole? You know exactly what you did." I looked at him. "He's not against you, Indy. He's not. Neither is the school. LC might have a few bad teachers, but it's the coolest school in the city."

"Are you done yet?"

"You shouldn't stay here. You know that."

He laughed. "Why not? This is my future, right? This is what they all see when they look at me, right? Fuck 'em, Tate, I don't care. I'll give 'em all what they want."

"He doesn't see that. The school might and other people might, but Dad doesn't. I don't."

He smiled, the glaze in his eyes still heavy. "You've always been the favorite, Tate. Always, man. Ever since we were little, you were always the one." He paused, looking away. "You're the one."

74

"Please, man. Come home. You know what this is, right?"

"What? My crappy life?"

"No. Things are totally out of control. And if it goes any further, neither of you will be able to make things better. It'll be the end."

He spit. "It was the end a long time ago. You just didn't see it."

I stared at my feet. "He just doesn't understand you, Indy. You're different than him, you know? And you go out of your way to prove it all the time. It's like you live for it."

He rolled his eyes. "I am soooo tired of hearing that shit. From you and Mom and everybody else besides him. Nothing but shit from him. That's what I get. I can't even wipe my ass without him telling me I did it wrong."

My pissed-off meter was rising, and I didn't want to get into it with him. "You're not coming home?"

"No. And I'm done with school."

"Fine. Fuck you, then."

He shrugged. "Oh well." Then he shut the door, and I stood alone on the stairs as the sun set and the dogs barked.

CHAPTER TEN

We sat at the dinner table, the three of us, and we might as well have been deaf-mutes. Dad rested his forearms on either side of his plate as he chewed, his fork clutched in his fist as he stared at his plate like some rain forest King Kong gorilla man. He'd stopped drinking, which was good, but the tension in the air made me think he was on the verge of exploding.

There was one person in the world who controlled my dad, and it was my mom. She knew how to talk to him and when to talk to him and when not to talk to him, and now she was silent. I couldn't be silent. I pictured Indy lying on Porkchop's couch, baked out of his mind and hating the world, and I couldn't stand it. It made me mad. "Can Indy come home?"

Dad the gorilla man kept his eyes on his plate. Mom looked at me and shook her head. "Not now, honey. Let's just eat our dinner."

My neck flushed. "No."

Dad's eyes rose from his plate. I swear to God his ears laid back and his neck swelled. He stared white-hot rivets into me. "Your mother asked that we not talk about this now."

"Dad, I just—"

His voice came low and dangerous. "Shut your mouth, Tate."

"I'm sorry." I paused. "I just don't think—"

Mom cut in. "Tate, please. We're all upset, and I think a little bit of time would do everybody some good."

I clenched my teeth. "Does that include Indy?"

Dad dropped his fork on his plate, leaned back, and ran his fingers through his hair. "What are you saying?"

I took a breath, then looked at my dad. "We can't talk about it because you'll get pissed, and since everything re-volves around you, I'm supposed to shut up," I said. I sat at the table, feeling like my words were coming from somebody else's mouth. Part of me screamed to shut up because this didn't happen in our house. We didn't talk like this to each other. Nobody did. But he didn't get it, and Indy was in trouble be-cause of it.

Dad's jaw muscles worked as he clenched his teeth. "Go to your room."

"He's my brother."

"I said go to your room."

"Or what? You'll hit me? I saw his face, Dad. Nice job."

Dad took a deep breath, his chest expanding. He put his elbows on the table, his fists under his chin. His knuckles were white. "You're taking this too far, son."

There was a warning in his eyes that I'd never seen until recently, but I couldn't stop myself from going on. "No, Dad, *you* took it too far."

Silence. Absolute silence.

Then he spoke. "You're right. But this isn't just about me. It's a struggle for your mother and me just like it's a struggle for you. And for Indy. I love him and care about him, but he needs to learn."

For some reason, I didn't accept what he said. Even though I knew it was true, I knew my dad's kind of love wasn't right for my brother. I looked at him, then stood up from the table. "That doesn't really matter right now, Dad."

He looked at me. "Where is he?"

I set my napkin on the table. "Baked out of his head trying to forget you," I said, then went to my room.

• • •

Mom came to my room an hour later. I could tell she'd been crying, and the stress lines on her face were tight. She leaned against the doorjamb. "Are you all right?"

"No. Are you?"

She sat on the end of my bed. "No. But I know everything will be all right."

I blinked, looking into her eyes. "You and Dad have no idea, do you?"

"About what?"

"About life. About Indy." I shook my head, frustrated.

"You guys think that sitting at a table every night eating dinner makes us some kind of all-American family. Yeah, you aren't divorced. Dad isn't a drunk. He doesn't beat you. You don't shoot meth. Great. But that doesn't change anything. Indy is in trouble, Mom, and Dad just doesn't get it."

She studied me for a moment. "Your father is holding things together the best way he knows."

"And you agree?" I said, shaking my head again.

A moment passed. "Yes, I do. And that may be hard for you to take. But Indy needs a strong hand. He's out of control." She smoothed the bedspread. "His school, the drugs, his attitude, everything, Tate."

I looked away. "I know, but I just don't get how kicking him out makes things better."

"He's not kicked out."

I looked at her. "Mom, Dad hit him."

"I know. And if he ever does again, he'll be alone."

I blinked. "You'd really leave him?"

She nodded. "You are my children."

I shrugged. "Why is he such a dick?"

She pursed her lips, thinking, and then she stood. "You'll understand when you're older, Tate. But we're doing everything we can," she said, leaning over and kissing the top of my head. "Tell your brother to come home. And tell him that I love him."

CHAPTER ELEVEN

I hate deadlines. But as I skated to school the next morning, I had a dead-line. Three days. If I didn't get Indy back home and back to school within three days, nothing would ever be the same again. He'd be expelled, the courts would come in, and Indy would never come home. Things would be too bad.

As I stuffed my board in my locker, a voice came from behind me.

"Tell me why I wouldn't understand."

I turned, and Kimberly Lawson stood there. I looked her up and down. "What?"

"You said that I wouldn't understand why beating some-body up and stealing could be good. Tell me why."

I grabbed my books. "Why should I?"

"Because I want to know."

"Keep on wanting to know, then." I walked down the hall.

She fell in beside me. "That's not fair. You brought it up."

"And you blew me off."

"I want you to tell me."

I stopped, facing her. "You want to know why I beat that guy up and took his money?"

She shook her head. "No. I want to know why you don't think I'd understand the reason you did it."

She had a few faint freckles on her nose. I shrugged. "You really want to know?"

"Yes."

"Okay, fine. Because you're a rich-girl superstar who does everything the world tells her to do without thinking about it. Bad is bad and good is good, and good means following all the rules no matter what. You don't understand anything else."

Her face cracked, and she looked to her feet. "You don't even know me."

"The only thing I need to know is how you looked at me yesterday." I hesitated, feeling a tiny bit guilty, but not that guilty. "So don't stand there and act like you're all high-and-mighty, because you don't know jack about why I do what I do."

She took a breath. "Okay, then. Tell me why there would ever be a good reason to beat up a guy and take his money."

I looked at the clock at the end of the hall. Two minutes until class. "He broke a little kid's board because he thinks his shit doesn't stink, so I made him pay for a new one. I even gave him his change. There. Happy?" Then I walked into class.

CHAPTER TWELVE

Sid and Piper sat on the concrete wall Under the Bridge smoking cigarettes after school, their boards on the ground beneath their feet. I hopped up next to Piper. "Seen Indy?"

Sid spit. "Are you ever not looking for Indy?"

"Bad stuff, guys. Indy's out of the house."

Piper nodded. "We know."

I looked across the park. "Three days suspended. Dad broke Indy's board and whacked him."

Sid grunted. "I might be the world's most pessimistic person, but I never figured your old man would do that."

I shrugged. "Things are messed up."

Piper frowned. "So, what do we do about it? Last two times I saw him, he was smashed."

"When did you see him?"

Sid hopped from the ledge. "Five minutes ago. He split. Said he didn't want to see you."

Piper hitched his thumb back to the skate park. "He's talking to Angie and her friend."

"Will?"

He nodded. "Uh-huh. Guy freaks me out. Never talks."

I shrugged. "Probably a raver like Angie."

Piper grunted. "She gives bad girls a good name, man. Nothing but trouble."

Sid shook his head. "She's got to be an alien."

Piper rolled his eyes. "Of course. That explains it."

Sid, his voice deadpan and serious, shrugged. "One of the genetically deficient alien species."

Piper laughed. "I forgot Earth was colonized by aliens."

Sid spit. "Whatever, man. I know, though."

Piper flicked his cigarette into the street, watching the butt smoke on the pavement. A car passed and crushed it. He glanced at me. "Indy told me he's not going back after the suspension."

I nodded. "Yeah."

Sid grunted. "Dude, did you see him carve the halls? That was so cool."

Piper took a swig of Gatorade, ignoring Sid. He knew Sid pushed my buttons sometimes. "Your dad really kicked him out, huh?"

I nodded. "Yeah, but he can come back now. My mom busted his nuts about it."

Sid smirked. "I would like to see the day *anybody* busts your dad's nuts."

"My mom is tough when she's pissed."

Piper shook his head. "Remember that time in fifth grade when he got mad at us for ruining your mom's roses? I pissed my bed every night for three months afterward."

I laughed, remembering. We'd pretended the roses were baseballs and whacked them with bats. "Yeah, but he was also the one who made us the mini-pipe three years ago. Spent, like, four days on the thing."

Sid almost smiled. "I learned more cusswords from him while he was building that than anybody else in the whole world. I owe him."

Piper nodded. "Once you get used to the scarier-than-shit thing, he's pretty cool."

I looked over my shoulder at the skate park, spotting Indy, then hopped down. "Be right back, huh?"

Sid whistled under his breath. I turned. "What, Sid?"

"Watch yourself, Tate."

"With what?"

Sid leaned back, hitching his thumb toward them. "I heard Will doesn't like you too much. I also heard he's setting up shop selling dope. He has a line from Texas. A big one."

A squirrel clawed at my belly. "So he is dealing?"

Sid nodded. "He caught up with Mike Thorburne over the weekend. Word is Will gave him a choice. Sell for him or end up in the hospital. Mike's his bitch now."

Piper looked across the park. "Why don't we head on over with you, Tate? Might be better that way."

I shook my head. "I don't have a problem with the guy. It'll be fine."

Piper saluted me as I turned and skated through the park. It wasn't too busy, with it being Tuesday. I ignored Angie and Will as I walked toward them, looking at Indy. "We've got to talk."

Indy studied my face for a moment. "Not in the mood, bro."

I glowered at him. "Get in the mood, then. You can't leave me hanging."

He craned his neck back, staring at the underside of the freeway for a few seconds, then focused back on me, smiling. "Still not in the mood."

"Come on, Indy."

Will looked at me. "He said he didn't want to talk."

I turned to Will. "I don't even know you. Back off."

He smiled, his eyes dark and sharp. "Or what?"

I tensed. "Listen, Will, I've got no problem with you. Leave it alone."

He stepped closer to me. "We've got business that's none of your business, so turn your ass around and walk away."

I looked at Indy. "So, you're dealing now? Is that it? Is that how you got the money for the board?"

Will moved between Indy and me, cocking his head at me. "I said leave."

I shoved him hard, sick of his mouth and his attitude. He flew back, almost falling as he grabbed the walkway handrail. I braced him, ready for what I knew would be a hell of a fight. It didn't come, though. He stood there studying me, no expression on his face except that wicked smirk and those eyes dead steady on me. His voice came soft and menacing. "You just made a big mistake."

For the first time in a long, long time, I realized I was facing a guy I *didn't* want to fight. There was something in those eyes that sent a chill down my spine, but I knew one thing. I wasn't leaving my brother because Will told me to. I had no choice. "Bring it, asshole."

Indy stepped forward, grabbing my arm. "Come on. I'll talk, Tate. Will, just leave it alone."

My eyes were locked on Will's, and after a moment, Indy pulled me away. He stared at the ground as we walked away. "Dude, what's the deal with you?"

I grabbed his shoulder and spun him around. "What's my deal? What's your deal? Why are you hanging with him? He's trouble, man. Not even fun trouble. Just scum."

He swallowed hard, shaking his head and looking away. "What do you want, Tate?"

"Why are you doing this? You're burning some major bridges here."

His face fell, and he shrugged. "Things change, and besides, I didn't do it. Dad did."

"Dad said you could come home."

"Well, I'm not."

"Why not?"

"Because I'm fine."

"You're fine high all the time and staying with a guy named Porkchop in a shitty trailer? That's fine?"

"I said I'm fine."

I shook my head, piecing things together. Will was hedging in on becoming a major player, and that meant trouble. "Is Porkchop dealing for him now?" I eyed him. "Sid told me Mike Thorburne is."

"I'm not staying with Chop anymore."

"Why?"

"He and Will don't get along, and when I told Chop we were buddies . . ." He paused, looking away. "Listen, Tate, I don't want to go home. Dad is just too much."

"Where are you going to stay?"

"Will said I could hang with him for a while."

"You are dealing, aren't you?"

Silence.

"You are, aren't you?"

He grunted. "Will asked me to mule some stuff for him, and I did. So what?"

I clenched my teeth. "Why?"

Indy dug in his pocket and fished out a hundred-dollar bill. He held it up, sneering at me. "That's why," he said.

"So you're going to be a drug dealer."

"Call it whatever you want, but I'm making money."

"Come on, Indy," I said, trying to reason with him. "So you don't like school. Big deal. What about your writing? What about skating? You know you could be pro one day, and the Invitational coming up could do it for you. They're offering sponsors if you win."

He looked at me for a moment, then smiled. "First of all, nobody gives a crap about my writing, and second"—he eyed me—"I can tell you've been jonesing to do the Invitational ever since we heard about it, and you could be the one to win. Not me."

"Don't do this."

He smiled, and something in his eyes, some kind of painful spite, swirled around like water going down a drain. "It's already done."

"What about Cutter? He's dead, Indy. And he's dead because of the crap you're muling now. That doesn't matter to you? We all had a deal. No more."

He looked at me. "You know what, Tate? I don't blame him for shooting up. This world sucks, and as far as I'm concerned, anything that makes it better is good." Then he left. I watched him walk back toward Angie and Will. There was nothing I could do, but I felt like I had to do something. I just didn't know what.

I went back to Sid and Piper, hopping up on the wall.

Piper looked over his shoulder, toward the park. "Bad news?"

"He's staying with Will."

Sid shrugged. "Looks like a parting of the ways."

"Shut up, Sid. This is serious."

Sid smirked. "Dude, Tate, calm down for once. Take a toke or something."

I clenched my teeth. "Sometimes you say just about the worst possible thing you could ever say."

Sid shrugged again. "Just saying. And by the way, I'm not smoking, but you're like a firecracker ready to explode. That's all. And it's not your fault that Indy is flaking off."

I faced him. "We're a crew. We take care of our own."

He looked away. "Listen, Tate, the only one around here who doesn't want to be part of the crew isn't here. It's his choice."

I clenched my teeth again. "Yeah, and remember those two guys in the park who gave you a hassle last summer? They had you down when I got there, Sid. Remember that? Remember who saved your ass a beating?" I stared, ice running through my veins. "Yeah. Me. That's no sweat, though, huh? You just take what you can get, right?" I shook my head. "Stick it up your ass, Sid. You're a dick." I stared at him. "He's part of the crew and he's in trouble. Just like Cutter was, and just like you've been. And if you don't get that, then maybe you should fuck off."

Sid was rock-steady, blunt and indifferent as usual. "He's making the choice, Tate. And maybe I will go fuck off, because I think you're being the dick."

Piper took a breath, cutting in. "You *are* on the edge, Tate. Like *dangerous* on the edge."

I kept my eyes on Sid. "No, I'm not."

Piper went on. "I know what you're thinking right now. That's on the edge."

My chest tightened. I felt like the whole world was against me. "Oh yeah? Then tell me what I'm thinking."

He swallowed. "You're thinking about beating the crap out of Sid, who you've known since you were six years old. That's not right, Tate. Not right at all."

I stared off in the direction Indy went, realizing Piper was right and I did feel like everything was out of control. I looked at Sid. "I'm sorry."

Sid nodded. "No sweat, Tate. You know how I feel about Indy. I'm just saying we all have choices."

I sighed. "Listen, I'm heading home. And I'm sorry. I've just got to get my head straight about this."

CHAPTER THIRTEEN

There was a silence around our house that usually wasn't there, like everybody was thinking and wondering the same thing but not talking about it. Indy was gone, but it was more than that. Mom didn't say three words to Dad all night, and I knew she was still mad at him. Dad just sat in front of the television staring at whatever show happened to be on. I passed through the living room and he was watching *Desperate House-wives*, which is so not my dad it could have been a joke. I wondered what was going on in his head, but thought better of asking.

I burrowed in our room, doing homework, reading a skate mag, then just staring at the ceiling thinking about Indy. I had a huge urge to blurt out that Indy was dealing, but I couldn't. Things would go from bad to worse, because I knew it came down to one thing. I didn't trust Dad. He'd go ballistic.

I decided not to say anything. Not now. Part of me was afraid Dad would stick to his guns, and another part of me was afraid it would mean him busting down Will's door and dragging Indy home. I didn't know what to do, and anger welled up in me.

I sat up and slung my legs over my bed, staring at Indy's side of the room. Indy. He should be here sitting at his computer and writing some story. I'd say something to him and he'd be so into the characters he wouldn't hear me, and then a couple of minutes later, he'd turn and ask me if I'd said something.

I thought about when we were kids. He'd always had a mouth, but it had been different then. Always joking and smiling and goofing around, having a good time. Always a million friends, too. He knew everybody because he wasn't afraid to know everybody. He could strike up a conversation with anybody and have them smiling thirty seconds into it, and people always just wanted to be around him. Indy was always the kid in the sun, flashing his teeth and egging you on to come have a good time. And I was always the guy making sure he was all right. I also envied him.

But it was changing, just like he'd said.

I stood, walking over to his desk and sitting in his chair. The screen saver scrolled geometric lines across the monitor, and I touched the mouse, the lines disappearing and his browser flashing on the screen. I clicked on Word, then Open, and looked at his files.

If Indy spent as many hours on his schoolwork as he did writing, he'd have already graduated college. But as I looked, I realized I'd had no idea just how much he'd done.

Forty documents—four novels and thirty-six short stories, ranging from ten pages to eighty, that he'd written in three years. I couldn't believe it. This was incredible, and not a single teacher had seen any of it.

I sat, staring at the files and not knowing where to start. I'd never even peeked into his computer before. Obviously, all those nights and weekends he'd spent sitting here had added up. I clicked on the first file.

. . .

At three-thirty in the morning, I'd been reading for over seven hours, rapt with attention as I scrolled through my brother's words and stories until I was brain-dead with fatigue. I hadn't even gotten to his novels. The last short story I'd read, his most recent, went deep, and I knew it was about him.

He'd made it fictional, but I could see right through his words and straight to how he felt about the world and school and us and himself. It wasn't sad or depressing or funny or disturbing, but all of them put together. Forty-one pages of my brother's feelings about life.

The story, called "Stealing Home," was about a baseball player who was good but never quite good enough, and his coach rode him hard about it, drilling it into his head about how to do things by the book and play by the rules and think like everybody else. He had to look right and play right and talk right, and if he didn't, well, he wouldn't be a good player.

He'd made the team and was popular and the world looked at him like he had it made, but he didn't feel that way. He knew he could do better, but something in him wouldn't let it happen. Some part of him rejected everything baseball stood for. He didn't care about trophies or winning or batting averages or any of the other things that made baseball what it was. From the time his cleats hit the clay to the time he stepped over that white baseline and went home, the only thing he wanted was to play for the sake of playing, not for the sake of winning. He loved it, but everything surrounding it made him hate it. And hate himself.

As I read, I finally understood. Baseball was school, and my dad and his teachers were the coach. And for Indy, lacing up those cleats was the same as sitting down at this computer and writing, except they had ruined it for him.

When I finished, I sat staring at the screen. My eyes burned and I was done for, but I couldn't stop thinking about it. The boy in the story—his name was Gregory—gave up baseball because of all the things that got in the way of playing. Just simply playing. His coach rejected him for being a quitter, and Gregory ended up jumping off the Monroe Street Bridge. Goodbye.

I sat back, worried over Gregory's fate and how it tied in to my brother. Indy had never said anything about suicide, and I couldn't see him doing it, but I couldn't keep my mind from it. Were things that bad? Was he really thinking about it?

It finally struck me. Indy *knew* what was going on, and he

knew what he was doing to himself. The spite that I'd seen in his eyes was ripping him apart.

My bro wasn't a rebellious teenager hell-bent on breaking the rules; he was breaking the rules because there was something in him that wouldn't let him follow them. I also had a feeling that he didn't *know how* to follow them. It just didn't click. But to kill himself? No. That wasn't my bro.

CHAPTER FOURTEEN

The next morning in first period, Mr. Bennett's phone rang, and my day went from crappy to nuclear crappy. Mr. Bennett stopped lecturing, picked up his phone, spoke for a moment, then hung up. "Tate, you're wanted at the office," he said, writing me a pass.

As I walked down the hall, I wondered what had happened now. I was exhausted after staying up all night reading, and didn't have much in me for more trouble. When I reached the office, I told the receptionist my name and she nodded, then directed me to my counselor's office.

I'd met her twice, both times for schedule mix-ups. Her name was Ms. Potter, and she'd seemed pretty cool. I knocked on the door, and she came to open it, smiling. "Come in, Tate."

I did. She took a seat behind her desk, squishing her chunky butt in the chair. She had a bob haircut, wore a necklace with huge plastic beads, and looked like she could be selling cookies at some church bake sale. I sat down across the desk from her.

"How are you today?"

"Fine."

"Good. I'm afraid I don't know you too well."

With every wrong thing going on right now, I knew this wasn't a getting-to-know-you meeting. "Why am I here?"

Her smile faltered. She took a breath. "Well, Tate, I wanted to talk to you about a couple of issues." She said *issues* with a sharp s, and it sounded odd. "How are things at home?"

Her pretty-cool status took an immediate dive. "None of your business, thanks."

She raised her eyebrows, then nodded. "Okay. Well, I just wanted to get in touch with you. You know, see how things were going."

I sighed. "Ms. Potter, you seem like a nice lady and all, but you can cut it with the bull. This is about my brother, right? Did my mom call?"

Surprised, she sat back in her chair. "I know about your brother, yes, but that's not what this is all about. And no, your mother didn't call." She looked at me for a moment. "It came to my attention that you recently beat up another student."

I tensed. "It was off-campus."

"Yes, I know. But since it was reported to me, and his injuries are . . . obvious, I wanted to talk to you."

I crossed my arms. "You can't bust me. Didn't happen here."

"I don't want to bust you."

"Who told you about it?" I asked.

She looked down at her desk. "That doesn't matter."

"Yeah, it does," I said.

She gazed at me. "Why would it matter?"

"Because if Corey came whining to you about it, I'll kick his ass all over again."

Her face hardened. "There's no need to threaten another student."

I blinked, thinking about what I'd done all night long, and how this place couldn't care less about my brother. "You know what, Ms. Potter? I don't really care what you think. You and everybody else here are nothing but hacks pulling a check." I stared at her. "Are we done?"

"Corey Norton did not report anything to me. And when I questioned him about it, he refused to talk."

"Good for him. Are we done?"

"Why did you beat him?"

I smiled. "A personal *issue*."

Silence. She was stumped. "I'm not your enemy, Tate."

"I don't think you are. But my problems are mine, and I know how this works."

"How does it work?"

"School policy says that I can get busted for fighting off-campus if you have a statement. You're not getting one. And you're not going to be able to add anything to whatever file you have on me or my brother."

She nodded, picking up my file and putting it in a desk drawer. "Okay, then. Let's forget that part. I won't ask about it, and I told you I had no intention of getting you in trouble."

"Then why am I here?"

"I think you are hostile and have anger problems. And that usually stems from other things happening in your life that aren't so good. I want to help you with those things if I can."

I smiled, sitting back. "Why? Because you know me so well?"

She continued, unfazed. "Why did you feel the need to use force?"

I shook my head. "You're not my shrink. Don't even start."

She took a breath. "Can I ask you a question, Tate?"

I shrugged. "Nothing has stopped you yet."

"When you hit him, did it feel good?"

I stood. "We're done. Bye."

CHAPTER FIFTEEN

The cool thing about Under the Bridge is that when it rains, you don't get wet. With thousands of tons of concrete and steel above your head, you have a good umbrella. Sid sat on the usual wall after school, chewing a wad of beef jerky. He kicked his heels against the brick. "Are you on steroids?"

I dropped my pack. "No."

"Are you going to beat me up?"

"No." I shrugged. "In fact, I was called to my counselor's office today to talk about my feelings of anger," I said, smirking.

"I figured. That's why I asked."

I looked at him. "You figured that I was going to be called down?"

He nodded. "Yeah. After I went and told Ms. Potter you were on the edge of apeshit, she said she'd talk to you." He held out his bag of dried meat. "Jerky?"

I stared, speechless.

"You said you wouldn't beat me up. No take-backs."

I snapped out of beat-Sid-up mode, taking a breath. "Why would you do that, man? I've got enough crap to deal with right now, and I don't need you ratting on me."

"Yeah, you do need me doing that. But I didn't rat on you. Ms. Potter is cool. I trust her," he said.

"Big mistake, Sid."

"You were right when you got pissed at me. We're a crew." He looked at me. "I may be weird and antisocial and all that other stuff, Tate, but I'm not stupid. You're heading toward some serious shit with Will and your bro and your family, and honestly, I'm afraid about it."

"Maybe, but you shouldn't have done that."

"I did do it. And I'm right. Will is different, man. He's hard-core, and if you two tangle, it won't be pretty."

"I can't believe you really went there."

"Just do me a favor, huh? Talk to her. She helped me with some stuff."

I took a breath, thinking about her question. Did it feel good to hit him? It'd been hounding me all day. "What did she help you with?"

"After Cutter died."

"Oh yeah?" I said, surprised.

He nodded. "Yes." He gazed up, staring at the underpass. "Sometimes I was just wishing I could get out, you know? Like him. Just end everything. My dad and his drinking, no money, all that crap. Not like I wanted to actually kill myself, but just that feeling you get in the morning. Like you really wished you didn't wake up. Like you could be . . . nothing."

"Jesus, Sid, you should have said something."

He shook his head. "I know what my life is, Tate, but she sort of helped me realize that it wasn't set in stone. That just because I was born weird and my life sucks in general, it didn't always have to be that way."

I smiled. "You are weird."

"I know. But that's not bad. Just something to deal with."

I looked at him. "She really helped you, huh?"

"I guess."

"Cool. And I'll think about it. Talking to her and stuff."

"Good, because I suck at this human stuff." An awkward moment passed. "Piper tells me you want in on the Invitational."

I hopped up on the ledge. "Thinking about it. You?"

"Naw. Not a corporate hack." He slid me a look. "No offense."

I laughed. "None taken."

He looked across the street, chewing his beef jerky. "Pipe wants to do it."

"Yeah."

"The rules state that first, you need a sponsor. Second, you need a team. At least three people. Teams compete, win or lose, and there'll also be an individual winner. That person gets a national sponsor."

"Yeah."

He nodded. "Get Badger to sponsor us and I'm in."

"Really?"

A smile lit up his face. "Of course I'm in. We're a crew, remember?"

I smiled, hitting his shoulder. "You know, Sid, you're not that bad after all."

"Don't get emotional."

"Sorry. Didn't think hitting you on the shoulder was emotional."

He shrugged. "First it's hitting, then the next thing is you trying to stick your tongue down my throat. I know how things work."

I laughed. "I'll just have to keep my feelings to myself. Just always know I want you."

He hopped from the ledge as Piper crossed the street. "Are we going to skate? I feel a romantic interlude coming on that I'm not too comfortable with."

As we set our packs on the concrete platform at the edge of the Monster, Corey and his crew showed up, saw us, and sat at the rails. Piper smiled, nodding to them. "Dude looks like a raccoon."

I threw Sid a look. "Be back in a minute," I said, heading toward them. Corey saw me coming and stood, the expression on his face uncertain. I lifted my chin at him. "Hey."

"Hey."

A moment passed, and I wondered why I was doing what I was doing. I cleared my throat. "How's the face?"

He didn't answer.

I sighed. "Listen, Corey, I might think you're a prick and a bully, but I shouldn't have done what I did."

He narrowed his bruised eyes at me. "So?"

I shrugged. "So I shouldn't have jumped on you so quick."

He studied me, licking his lips. "This some sort of joke?"

I clenched my jaw. "Take it how you want it, but no, it's not. And it's not an apology, either. You're an asshole. But I shouldn't have jumped you so quick."

He blinked, studying my face. "Okay."

CHAPTER SIXTEEN

The next day before school, after another evening of pins and needles in the house, I grabbed my board and pack and headed down to room 143. Mrs. Nelson was Indy's English teacher, and she sat behind her desk talking to a student when I came in. She made eye contact with me as she talked, so I stood to the side for a few minutes until the conversation was over.

Mrs. Nelson was in her mid-fifties, and though I'd never had her, I'd heard she was hard. She turned to me as the other student left. "May I help you?"

I nodded, stepping to her desk. "I'm Tate Brooks. Indy's brother. He's in your class third period."

Her eyes darkened. "He does occasionally come to my class."

"He's suspended right now."

"I am aware of that." She smiled, but it wasn't a friendly smile. More sarcastic than anything. "I suppose you're here to get his homework?"

"No." I dug in my pack, ignoring the jab, and took out

"Stealing Home." "I was wondering if you could read this. He wrote it. I think it's good."

She looked at it as I held it out to her. "Is it an assignment? We're working on essays right now. I believe he has two that have not been turned in. Of course, along with just about every other assignment this semester."

"No. It's just something he wrote. A story. He loves writing."

She didn't take it. "I'm sorry, Mr. Brooks, but I don't have time to be entertained with something written by a student who doesn't care enough to attend my class, let alone complete the assignments I hand out."

I nodded. "I know, but if you could just . . . he writes all the time, and I think if you read it, you'd like it."

She pursed her lips, irritated. "Perhaps your brother should concentrate on what work he does have if he expects to get anywhere useful in his life. He's welcome to come see me anytime to speak about the matter."

I tucked "Stealing Home" back in my pack. "Whatever."

"Excuse me?"

I stared at her. "Fuck you, lady." Then I left.

• • •

"Yeah, I did."

Ms. Potter looked at me. "Why?"

I looked back at her. I wasn't about to gush about taking Indy's story to Mrs. Nelson. "Because she's a bitch."

She took a breath. "I talked to Vice Principal Poppe, and she's agreed to let you out of detention."

I furrowed my brow. "Why? I told a teacher off."

"I told her I'd get you to see me instead. For anger-management sessions."

I laughed. "I'll take detention."

"Did you think about my question, Tate?"

I paused, not sure I wanted to get into this. "Yes."

"And?"

"Yeah, it felt good. And yes, I wanted to hit him."

"Do you think that's good to feel that way?"

"I think he deserved it."

"That's not what I asked. Is it good for you to feel rewarded by causing pain to another person?"

I shook my head, frustrated. "No, and I know what you're getting at. I'm not some psycho who gets off on hurting people. It's just . . . ," I said, looking away. I'd never really thought about it like this, and it was disturbing. "It's just that it makes it stop, you know?"

She shook her head. "I don't know."

I shrugged. "It makes it stop. All the shit in this world. All the people who should do the right thing but don't. You can't talk them into it. It's easier to just make them."

"So forcing them through violence makes them do the right thing?"

I looked at her. "The kid got a new board, didn't he? Tell me that isn't right."

"That may be true, but do you think there could have

been a peaceful way to solve the problem? Maybe through proper channels?"

"Don't give me the no-violence bullshit, okay? It might work in your little world, but it doesn't work in mine."

She leaned forward on her desk, her palm under her chin. She fiddled with a pen. "If the police had been contacted, they would have contacted his parents and the school. It would have been moderated, and a solution could have been reached, including punishment."

I smiled. "I solved the problem in three minutes."

She sat back, frustrated. "So we should all just go around beating up people we disagree with? Come on, Tate, you're smarter than that. You're not a brute. I know it."

For the first time, the real person seemed to come through, and for some stupid reason, it meant something to me. "I talked to him."

"Who?"

"Corey. Told him I shouldn't have jumped him so quick."

She blinked, then smiled. "Wonderful."

I shook my head. "Not really. Just makes it easier for douche bags like him to keep pulling stuff."

"Then why did you talk to him?"

I looked away. "Because I know you're right, but some-times things just can't be that way."

• • •

On the way home, I noticed flashing lights down the alley adjacent to the skate park. Yellow police tape cordoned off the entrances, and several police cars, an ambulance, and two unmarked cars surrounded the area. A news crew filmed off to the side of the scene, and I stopped where a group of skaters were watching.

I stood next to Billy Oliver, a sophomore I'd seen around the park. "What's up?" I asked.

"Found a dead guy behind a Dumpster."

"Bum?"

He shook his head. "Nope," he said, pointing to two detectives questioning a kid. "Alex Larson found him."

Trepidation filled me. "Who was it?"

"Lucius. Deal went bad, I guess. Beat to death."

I furrowed my brow. "Any word on who did it?"

He shook his head. "None, but it was pretty brutal."

I nodded. "Looks like things will change around here, then," I said, my mind swimming.

CHAPTER SEVENTEEN

I skated the sidewalk in front of the field house after talking with Ms. Potter and watched as a busload of girls from another high school piled off and streamed inside, blocking my way. They wore volleyball uniforms. I thought of Kimberly Lawson.

As the last girl filed off the bus and the coach followed them in, I kicked my board up, strapped it to my pack, and went inside. Up a twenty set, to the left, and down a carpeted hall found me at the doors to the gym. I peeked inside, and the stands were filling with students and parents while the Lewis and Clark varsity team warmed up, bumping and setting and spiking as their opponents put their bags down and got ready. This was a different world than mine, that was for sure.

I stood at the doors as people hustled by, and found Kimberly on the court, her dark hair pulled back in a ponytail as usual. She looked like every other long-legged chick on the court hitting balls over the net. Black shorts, knee pads, tennis shoes, orange and black jersey, hair pulled tight. Just as I was about to walk back out, she looked up and saw me. She stared for a moment, then smiled before the coach yelled at her for missing her turn.

I walked in and found a seat on our team's side. I'd never watched a volleyball game in my life, and it took me a while to figure out that you couldn't score a point unless your team served the ball, but it was cool.

Kimberly was an awesome player, and after a few good saves where she dove in and bumped the ball up for another player to get, I found myself caught up in the game, cheering the team on. They were playing Mead, which had a good team. I heard the fans around me talking about a championship if they could take them out, and the tension was high enough that I thought I might have a feeling of school spirit.

By the end of the game, Kimberly had made a bunch of aces when she served the ball, which meant that nobody on the other side was able to return it. I felt like a complete goofball not knowing anything. I didn't even know how long they would play, if there were quarters or halves or periods. But I had a good time. A strange good time. I almost felt like an alien in my own school; schools don't have much use for skaters, and because of that, skaters don't have much use for school.

LC won, and with the last serve capping the game, the crowd stood and cheered, going apeshit. I watched as the girls celebrated on the court, then gave the other team a cheer,

and the coach huddled with them for a talk. People were filing out of the gym, and I stood, looking for Kimberly on the
sidelines. When I found her, she was hugging her dad. He was
totally beaming. Our eyes locked for just a moment before she
focused back on the celebration, and a smooth river of electricity ran through me. I smiled, shaking my head at why I felt
the way I did, and then I left.

I skated through the park on the way home, looking
for Indy, wanting to talk to him about Gregory in "Stealing Home." He wasn't around, so I split, and I wasn't really
in the mood to skate anyway. By the time I got home, Mitchell
the grom was sitting on our front porch. "Hey, Mitch. How's
the deck?"

He smiled. "Great."

"So, what's going on?"

He sniffed, scrunching his nose up, then picking it. He
flung a booger. "Awww, just around, you know?"

Then I remembered. "The trucks. That's right. They're in
the garage. Just a second and we'll stick 'em on." I opened the
door and dropped my pack in the entry, calling out to Mom.
No answer. She must have been in the salon with a late client. I went back out, waving for Mitch to follow me around to
the driveway.

As I slid the garage door open, Will's beat-up old station
wagon pulled up and Indy got out. I straightened as my bro
came down the driveway. "Hey, Indy."

He looked tired. Dark bags under his eyes made him look
strung out, and his hair was greasy. He wore a new gold neck-

lace. Real gold. He smiled. "Hey, bro." He looked at Mom's car. "Mom inside?"

I shook my head. "Late client. In back." Dad had built a small, one-room building for Mom to do hair in, and she'd been developing a clientele for a while now, working more.

"Cool."

"You look like hell."

He grinned. "Thanks."

I smiled. "You coming home?"

He shook his head. "Getting some stuff. Clothes and crap."

"Oh."

He stood there for a moment looking at me, then smiled at Mitch. "Hey, shrimp."

"Hey. You going to the Pro Skater Invitational?"

Indy furrowed his brow, like he'd forgotten. "Here?"

Mitch smiled. "Yeah. End of next week at the arena. They're setting up the whole floor. Huge pipe, man, bigger than the Monster. It's gonna be on national TV." He burped. "They're also letting local guys skate after the pros, but only sponsored. Top guy wins, top crew wins."

Indy rolled his eyes. "Sorry. Not for me."

Mitch looked at me. "You going?"

I thought about Piper wanting to go sponsored. "I don't know. Maybe."

Mitch smiled again. "My dad said he'd buy a ticket for me if I worked every day after school. I'm going." He looked at us. "We could go together, huh? The whole crew or something, right? That would be bangin'."

Indy shrugged, sliding me a glance. "Not interested, man. Sponsored guys blow. Listen, I'm grabbing my stuff and jetting. Take it easy." Then he left, walking around the corner of the house to the front door.

I grabbed the trucks out of a drawer and set them on the driveway, then began unscrewing Mitch's old ones from his deck. I glanced at Will in the station wagon. He took a drag from a smoke, then flicked the butt on our driveway. I stood. "I'll be back in a minute, Mitch. Hang on."

He grabbed the screwdriver and the wrench. "Sure. I can get the others off."

"Good deal." I walked down the driveway toward Will, then thought better of it, turning and going to our front door.

I found Indy in our room, stuffing clothes in a bag. "Hey."

He continued stuffing. "Hey."

"I read some of your stuff."

He kept his head down. "Stay out of it. It's not yours."

I looked at him. "I read 'Stealing Home.'"

He paused, said nothing, then went back to packing.

"It's you, isn't it? Gregory is you."

He concentrated on his bag. "It's none of your business, Tate."

"Yeah, it is my business."

He straightened. "What, then? What do you have to say?"

"Gregory killed himself."

"It's a story. That's all."

"It might be a story, but you feel like him, don't you?"

He zipped his bag. "No, I don't. I'm not Gregory. Gregory wasn't smart enough to get out. I'm getting out."

"So this is how you get out? By living with a drug dealer and muling his dope like street trash?"

He clenched his jaw. "Back off, Tate."

"No."

He looked at me, his eyes hard and cold. "Take it easy." He picked up his bag, slinging it over his shoulder and looking at me. "I'm done with this shit, and I'm done with you telling me what to do." He tried to shoulder past me, but I blocked his way. His eyes flashed. "Get out of my way, Tate."

I knew we were about to go over the line together. The last time we'd mixed it up physically had been in fifth grade. I backed off, Ms. Potter heavy in my mind. "Indy, just think about it. Come home. This is killing Mom, Dad is messed up, and Cutter . . ."

His eyes met mine. "You can take your guilt trip and shove it up your ass, okay? I'm leaving." Then he pushed me out of the way, heading for the door.

I called to him, "If you weren't Gregory, you'd face your problems, Indy."

Indy stopped, turning. "Then tell me this, Tate. Has he asked about me? One single word since I've been gone?"

I had nothing to say.

He smirked, then gave me the finger. "Give that to him for me." Then he was out the door.

When I came out, he was just getting in the station wagon. Will grinned at me as he drove away.

I walked around the house, preoccupied and pissed off. Mitch was putting his trucks on. He smiled. "These are awesome. You want money for them?"

"Don't worry about it." I sat cross-legged on the driveway, my mind on Indy. "So you're going to the Invitational?"

He picked his nose, flicking another booger on the pavement. "It costs twenty-five bucks. Dad said he'd pay for it, though."

"Cool."

Mitch tightened the last nuts. "Too bad you and Indy aren't sponsored. You'd win." He stared at his board. "Just imagine skating with the pros. Killer. I'd do it."

I blew it off, even if it did sound cool. I studied his board. "Looks good. Those trucks set right?"

He tested them. "Yeah. You in a fight with Indy?"

"Sort of."

He put the finishing touches on the wheels, tightening them just enough to give some play. "Man, I wish I had a bro. We'd never fight. We'd be buds, man. Skate all day."

"No brothers or sisters?"

"Two half sisters. They come for a couple of weeks in the summer. They're weird, though. From Louisiana."

I smiled. "People from Louisiana are weird, huh?"

"Yep. Not as weird as Sid, though. They got alligators there, you know? And they talk funny and eat weird things." He did an ollie. "Perfect."

I smiled again. "Cool."

He kick-flipped. "Awesome. Thanks."

"No sweat. Take it easy."

"Wanna skate?"

"Not today. Sorry."

He nodded. "You shouldn't fight with your bro, Tater. That's stupid." Then he was skating down the driveway, waving over his shoulder.

CHAPTER EIGHTEEN

When my parents fight, they do everything they can to make it seem like they're not fighting. When I was little, it was easy, but when your mom and dad talk to everybody except each other, you start noticing as you get older.

At dinner that night, Mom talked to me, and Dad wasn't as silent as the night before and asked me how my day went, but neither of them said a word to each other unless it was "please" or "thank you" for passing the mashed potatoes or corn.

There was a huge invisible elephant named Indy Brooks in our house, and nobody wanted to see it. Nobody wanted to see him. Not my dad or mom or anybody who should have. Nobody knew what to do, and it burned me up. After dinner, I grabbed my jacket and board, and Dad looked up from fixing a lamp on the dining room table. "Where are you going?"

"Out."

"Where?"

"Out."

He glanced at the clock. Nine forty-five. "It's too late."

"What do you care?"

"Well, for one, I saw on the news that a scumbag drug dealer was murdered behind O'Malley's pawnshop." He eyed me. "You spend a lot of time down there. I don't think it's a good idea."

"It doesn't matter what you think," I said, my insides quivering.

He set his electrical tester down. "What did you just say to me?"

I shrugged. "I'm going out, and you can't stop me."

He bristled, standing. "Don't, Tate."

"Oh, so you care about one son but not the other, huh?"

Dark clouds gathered in his eyes. "Don't start with that, Tate. You know—"

I shook my head. "No, I don't know."

He jabbed a thick finger at me. "You are going to sit your ass down right now and we'll talk about it. Got it?"

"No. We don't talk in this house. You talk. You just ram it down Indy's throat until he can't take it anymore. That's all you do."

"That's not true. . . ."

I shook my head again. "I saw him today, if you're interested." I paused, looking at him. Indy's words—*Has he asked about me? One single word*—stung me, and anger overwhelmed the fear of disrespecting my father. "He told me to give this to you." Then I flipped him off.

I hadn't noticed, but Mom had heard us talking and come

from their room. Dad stared at me, stunned as I held my finger toward him. His neck muscles bunched, but Mom cut in. "You're going to see him, aren't you?"

I lowered my finger, my eyes still locked on his. "Yes."

Her voice was soft but commanding. "Be careful, then."

Dad stood silent, Mom's invisible harness keeping him at bay. With one more look his way, I left.

Will's apartment building, the Coldstone, was almost three miles from our house, and by the time I got there it was almost ten-thirty. The Coldstone sat on Third Avenue on the west end of the downtown area, and it wasn't known for a welcoming atmosphere unless you were looking for something on the dark side of things. Dingy bars, taverns, run-down porno shops, winos, drunk rednecks, whores, pimps, and dealers littered the streets like discarded and broken junk in a dump. As I skated down the sidewalk, a police cruiser slowly passed by, the cop eyeing three scruffy guys standing outside a tavern called Burt's.

I made my way to the end of the block, to the Coldstone, and went in the lobby. A huge lady in a flowered muumuu sat on one of the benches near the elevators, and I walked over. She held a Big Gulp, and a basket with a potted flower sat on the floor at her feet. I smiled, not interested in why a four-hundred-pound woman would be carrying a potted flower at ten-thirty at night. "Hi."

She had a sheen of sweat on her forehead, and she dabbed at it with her wrist. "Hello." I punched the up button even though she already had. She grunted. "Slow elevators. This building is older than our blessed Lord himself."

I watched as the dial lowered from floor to floor. "Yeah."

"I tried to get a ground-floor place because of my condition, but I couldn't. It's a glandular thing. Genetical. My doctor said I could probably sue this place under the Americans That Are Disabled Act because I'm handicapped, but they're nice here. Told me I'd get the very next ground-floor vacancy, they did, and said that old man Kentucky Jim is about to expire. Drunk himself out of a liver, he did. Not to say that I'd want him to die at all, the poor man, but he does have a ground-level."

I waited. "Cool." The doors finally opened and we got on, me holding the doors open for her while she waddled inch by inch into the cubicle. "What floor?"

"Six. Thank you, dear." I pressed six, then three. Will's apartment was 322. The elevator ground its way up, me looking up like an idiot and the lady staring at me. "Are you new here?"

I shook my head. "Visiting."

She laughed. "That's probably a good thing. The last place I lived was worse, though. The water came out brown for the first few seconds when you turned on the tap, and my neighbor, Lordy Lordy, he was always banging around and fighting with his girlfriend. Horrible, horrible. And my gosh, when they would have . . . uh, relations, it was so loud I almost felt like I was in the room with them. Not that I need a boyfriend or anything like that or would want to be in there, but I'm just telling you."

"Gotcha. That sucks." I stared at the buttons, and finally, the door opened on the third floor. We said goodbye to each other, and as the doors closed I looked at the apartment number across the hall. It was 315. I walked down the hall, realized I was going the wrong way, then turned around, backtracking to near the end of the hall and finding the right number.

I stood there for a moment before knocking, wondering what I was going to find and almost turning back. I'd come this far, and when I got home to Dad ready and waiting to flay me alive, hopefully I'd have Indy with me so I could avoid it. I knocked, covering the peephole with my finger. No answer, so I knocked again. A few seconds later, the door swung open.

An older guy, probably around forty and with tightly parted and thinning hair, answered the door. Clean-shaven and wearing worn slacks and a faded blue polo shirt to match, he furrowed his brow at me. He stuffed a stack of credit cards in his back pocket. "What do you want?"

I looked over his shoulder, trying to see if Will was there. I wasn't sure I had the right place. "Uh, I'm looking for Indy."

"Who are you?"

"His brother. I need to see him."

"He's not here."

"Where is he?"

"I'm not his babysitter, kid." He went to shut the door, and I put my hand up, holding it open. His eyes flashed to my hand. "You don't want to do that."

"Sir, I need to find my brother."

He smiled. "You'd better get your hand off that door before I take it off for you."

I kept my hand there. "I just need to talk to him. It's important."

"He's out."

I sighed. This was going nowhere fast, and by the looks of him, he was about to take my hand off the door and most likely rip it from my arm, too. I stepped back. "Would you mind telling him Tate stopped by?"

He smiled again. "Sure thing. And by the way, coming by here again wouldn't do you too much good. Got it?"

I didn't want to wait for the elevator, so I took the stairs, quickstepping down to the lobby and walking outside. The night was cool, almost crisp, and I stood there wondering what to do as I watched a lady standing on the corner hustling money. She wore thigh-high black vinyl boots with huge heels, a short denim skirt, and a tight top, and she had the pudgy look of a person who ate fast food every day. A feather boa wrapped around her shoulders fluttered in the breeze.

I put my board down, sitting on it and leaning my back against the brick of the Coldstone.

She turned, smiling. "Wanna good time, honey?"

I shook my head. "No thanks."

"Your loss." She smirked, then faced the street, showing her wares.

A few minutes passed before a shiny white SUV with a middle-aged man in it crept past, then braked and backed up. The lady went up to the passenger window as it rolled down, talked to the guy for a minute, then hopped in. Around the corner they went, and I was alone.

Fifteen minutes later, she walked around the corner, apparently finished with her job. She took her place at the curb, then spoke, her back to me. "Waiting for something or no place better to go?"

I looked at her cottage-cheesy butt. "Waiting."

Her eyes scanned the road as she talked. "What's your name?"

"Tate."

She laughed. "I wonder what a boy named Tate would be waiting for in a part of town like this."

"My brother."

"Runaway?"

"Sort of."

She twirled her boa. "I ran away once. Never came back, either."

I looked at the profile of her face as she watched cars drive by. "Where'd you go?"

She laughed again. "Honey, after two weeks of running through every friend I had, I came here."

"How long ago was that?"

"Five years."

I crossed my arms over my chest, cold as the night deepened. "How old are you?"

"Nineteen."

I looked at her. She'd been a prostitute since she was fourteen. She looked old. I'd thought at least twenty-seven or twenty-eight. "I'm almost seventeen."

She grunted, waving to a car. "Age don't matter here, honey. Time does. Get your brother out of here if you can."

Just then, a police car rolled up and the passenger window rolled down. The cop, with a thick mustache and black hair, shook his head. "Move along, Mindy. Call it a night or I'll take you in."

She smirked. "Come on, Jack. One more and I'll pay my rent."

"Move it or lose it, girl."

She sighed, staring down the street, then looked at me. "Hope you find your brother, Tate. Good luck."

"Yeah, thanks," I said, watching her walk around the corner.

The cop idled his car, eyeing me. "New to this area, son?"

"No. I mean, I'm just waiting for my dad. He's working late tonight." I looked down the street, seeing a plumbing truck parked at the curb in front of Burt's Tavern.

He stared at me, suspicious. "Where does he work?"

I hitched my thumb to the Coldstone behind me. "He's a plumber. Some kind of busted pipe or something." I pointed. "There's his truck. A-1 Plumbing. Heard of it?"

He shook his head. "Can't say I have, but there's no loitering around here. I'll give you twenty minutes; then you'll have to go inside when I come back around."

"Thanks."

He rolled on then, and I waited. Three drunks rambled out of the tavern, one of them puking on the side of the building before they made their way down the sidewalk, talking about some bitch in the bar with curly hair. I leaned my head back on the brick wall and looked up, wondering how much longer he'd be.

The cop came back on his rounds twenty minutes later, and as I saw his cruiser come down the street, I walked around the corner, set my board to pavement, and skated. Halfway home I kicked my board up and walked.

This late, there was hardly any traffic and fewer people out. As I passed under the humming buzz of fluorescent lights on a pawnshop sign around the corner from the skate park, a guy in a midnight-blue Acura pulled up beside me and rolled his passenger window down. "Got anything?"

I shook my head, not stopping but knowing what he wanted. "Around the corner. Far end of the park."

He nodded, slowly rolling around the corner. As I turned up toward the park, I watched as the Acura sat in the shadows Under the Bridge, the dim figure of a dealer at his window handing him his dope. Five seconds later, the car drove away.

I crossed the street to distance myself from whoever was there, putting my board down and skating. As I passed, I kept my eyes straight and forward. Night people and street people and partiers were one thing, but if you didn't treat the dealers like they were ghosts, you drew attention to yourself, and that was a bad thing. Unless you bought dope, that is.

I glanced back as a pickup truck with a broken muffler pulled up. Out of the shadows came the dealer, and I stopped, kicking my board up and turning on my heel. I reached the spot Under the Bridge just as the truck pulled away and the dealer was walking back into the shadows. I raised my voice, and it echoed under the cavernous vault of concrete. "He got it from here."

Indy turned around, his eyes wide as he stuffed bills in his pocket. He said nothing, just stared at me.

I walked up to him, dropping my board and grabbing the front of his shirt, my face inches from his. "You know it, right? That night. Cutter got his stuff right here from a guy just like you. Scum. Trash."

His breath was warm on my face as he spoke. "So, you're going to beat me up, huh?"

A long moment passed, our eyes searching each other, and all I could think of was Cutter. He'd died in my arms, his glazed eyes on mine as his heart took its last beat. I clenched my teeth, shoving Indy back. "You're not fucking worth it, you traitor."

It took a moment for what I said to register with him. Four years of watching the dealers from the other side of the park sell to addicts flashed through my head, and now he was here. We were here. He was one of them. We'd all made a pact that we'd never deal and that we'd never do the hard stuff. Indy, me, Sid, and Piper. Now I was standing under the wrong side of the bridge talking to my drug-dealer brother. He'd betrayed me, but most of all, he'd betrayed himself. His face went blank, and then he nodded. "You don't understand, Tate. Just go home. Please."

A moment passed between us, and it seemed that in a few seconds' time, the only thing I had left of my brother was remembering how it used to be. He was right. Things had changed, and I hated it. I hated the world and my dad, and most of all, I hated my brother because he was the only one who could hurt me like this. "Fuck you, Indy." Then I was gone.

• • •

On the way home, my mind rushed through things. We didn't live in an insulated world. Guys I'd known living further up the hill, with a buffer of space and money, didn't think like we did. They didn't know what we knew. They didn't see what we saw. There was no buffer with us because we were the buffer that kept it from other people. Our neighborhood was the zone that separated the city from the suburbs, and you dealt with what it threw you because there was nothing else to do.

I knew the drug world because I saw it every day. I skated through it. I knew the dealers and the pimps, the badasses, gangbangers, and thieves. I knew where to go and where not to go, who to talk to and who not to talk to, and how the game was played. The street was a tapestry, and we knew it. But we weren't the street. We never had been, and we knew the difference. We also knew that if it got to you, it sucked you in. It ruined you.

Over the last couple of years, we'd seen guys sucked in by it. Dealing, doing, thieving, joining gangs, getting involved with the wrong people. Now my own brother was in it, and I didn't know what to do. Part of me said he wasn't in too deep and I could get him out, but another part was so pissed off I didn't want anything to do with him. My brain boiled over with it all the way home.

Dad was sitting on the front porch when I came up the walk. It was after two in the morning. He reminded me of a great, hunch-shouldered statue of a bear—a warning to anybody crossing the doorway to his cave. I stopped five feet in front of him, far enough away that if he rushed me, I could run.

A few seconds passed; then his voice, low and soft, vibrated through the air. "Go to bed."

I did.

CHAPTER NINETEEN

Dad was gone on an early shift before I got up, and that was just fine with me. Usually a good night's sleep rearranged my attitude when it was swirling down the toilet, but I woke up in a worse mood than I went to bed with. I was sure the shit was going to hit the fan when he got home that night, and part of me envied my brother not having to deal with it.

I was still so mad at Indy that even thinking about him made my blood boil, and as I brushed my teeth, I thought about what Mom had said about Dad the other night. I stopped brushing, looking at myself in the mirror. Am I him? I thought. Am I my dad? I looked at myself hard for a moment more, then spit in the sink. I was so pissed at Indy I could beat his face in, and it was because I cared about him, no matter how much I didn't want to. I didn't know what to do, either, and that made me more angry. Ms. Potter might have been right, but I realized that sometimes, being right isn't enough.

• • •

School dragged on with my mind in the nowhere zone, and when lunch came around, Sid came along with it. I sat on the concrete wall eating a bag of chips, and he sat next to me, not saying hello or even looking at me. "Word on the down-low is all about your bro."

"Oh yeah?"

He nodded. "He's dealing Under the Bridge."

I looked across the street, wondering if there was a hole I could crawl into. "Yeah."

Sid shrugged. "Not just the light stuff, either."

I turned to him. "What do you know about Will?"

He shrugged again. "He's the real thing."

I told him about the guy at the apartment, and that he was holding a stack of credit cards.

He nodded. "Doesn't surprise me. That stuff goes hand in hand."

"He's in deep, Sid."

He sighed, kicking his heels against the wall. "Dangerous deep. I was talking to Michael about Will. I guess Will's uncle has ties from Texas. Was he sort of older?"

"Yes."

"He came up about a week ago. He supplies Will. Some sort of convict."

• • •

After sixth period let out, I had no plans to hit the park. Indy dealing was something I didn't want to answer to, and I knew I'd have to put up with questions. It was embarrassing, and if there was one thing I couldn't stand, it was being ashamed.

I couldn't escape it, though, and when I got home, Piper was sitting on our front porch. He stood, slapping me five. "Hey, Tate."

"What's up?"

He shrugged. "So what do we do about Indy dealing?"

I sighed, sitting down. "I don't know. I don't even know if I should tell my parents. My dad would go off the charts."

"This isn't about your dad, dude. It's about Indy."

"So I should tell him?"

"I don't know, but it's not about your dad."

I thought about it. "I could waste Will. Scare him off."

"I don't think he's the kind of guy who would scare off because you beat him up. I think it would escalate." He paused. "Besides, Indy's doing it because he wants to, not because Will is making him."

"Yeah. I just can't believe it. After Cutter and everything," I said, my thoughts trailing off.

Piper took a breath, pausing. "The law came to my house last night."

I glanced at him. "Why?"

"Lucius."

I frowned. "What do you have to do with Lucius?"

He shrugged again. "They said they're questioning all the

skaters who hang there. Looking for clues or whatever." He looked at me, and a long moment passed.

"What?" I said.

He eyed me, nervous tension on his face. "Come on, Tate, I know you've thought about it."

"About what?"

"Lucius. Dead. Will running dope Under the Bridge. Your bro."

I had thought about it, but I didn't want to even consider the consequences. "They said it was a bad drug deal."

He shook his head. "I know, and I'm not saying anything, but it's there. And I was questioned about it."

"Shit."

He nodded. "There's a videotape."

"Of the killing?"

"Sort of. They showed it to me. The pawnshop has had break-ins, so they have a surveillance camera on the back of their building. You can see two guys, just shapes in the dark, really, talking. Then one of them swings something and the other one goes back, falling out of the camera view. The other guy goes after him."

"So what? Do the cops think you did it?"

"Cops think everybody is a suspect, but they were just asking questions about anything I might have seen around. Pretty standard crap, I think."

"And?"

He frowned. "And I didn't say anything. About Will or Indy. But there was more."

"More?"

He nodded again. "As the tape is rolling, this detective dude pushes the zoom on his laptop and zeroes in on the back corner of the frame. There's a shape there, Tate. Another dude." He looked at me. "A witness."

"Who?"

"They don't know. Too fuzzy and dark."

I remembered the guy at Will's apartment. "Maybe Will and his uncle did it."

"Who knows. Lucius had problems with bangers up north, too. At least that's what the word was."

I took a breath. "I suppose they'll end up coming here to question me, too."

He nodded. "Yeah, which makes two big problems."

"Explain."

"Well, first off is that Indy is dealing down there, and with the investigation, the cops will eventually find out. The second is that Will and his uncle are serious people."

I knew he was right. "You didn't say anything about Indy?"

"Nothing. He's got enough problems without me snitching him out as a dealer."

"Thanks."

He picked up his board. "No sweat. Take it easy."

• • •

I had two goals for the night. One was to avoid my dad and the other was to find Indy. I had to talk to him. Dad was the obstacle, though, because when he did talk to me, he was totally cool. No threats, no hard-core, no grounding. Every bone in my body screamed to tell him what was going on, but I couldn't. Not yet.

After a mostly silent dinner, I went to my room, and a few minutes later he knocked. "Come in."

He walked in, dwarfing Indy's computer chair as he sat. "I want to talk about what's going on."

"Okay."

He took a moment, then began. "I know you're upset about Indy, and I know you love him. I do, too. And I know that in some ways, your loyalties lie closer to him than they do to me. I appreciate that, and I understand it. But this is my house, Tate, and there's got to be rules. And respect. Your brother didn't follow the rules, and he pushed it to the point where I had to do something about it." He paused, leaning his elbows on his knees and steepling his fingers. "If you don't like what I did, you have every right to tell me and we can argue about it. But you don't have a right to disrespect me or your mother because you're upset." He looked at me. "You didn't respect me last night or even the other night, and everything I said holds true. I will not tolerate it in my home, and if you choose to behave this way, you'll pay my consequences. Do you understand where I'm coming from?"

I did, and he was right. "I'm sorry."

He stood. "Don't apologize to me, Tate. Apologize to your mother. You and I can go in circles just fine, but your mother . . ." His eyes flared. "She's not your mother when it comes to those things, Tate. She's my wife."

I looked at him, and I realized he saw me as a man. Not

a kid, not a child, but a man. I nodded. "It won't happen again."

He nodded.

"I think you were wrong about Indy."

"I know you do, and I might have made a mistake, but Indy can own up to his mistakes just as I can to mine." He walked to the door, and once again I was surprised at how savvy he was. "I know you're probably going out tonight to see your brother, and that's fine. Tell him he's welcome home to iron things out at any time. And tell him I love him."

CHAPTER TWENTY

Under the Bridge. As I skated down the hill, the streetlights bathing me in a midnight glow as I rolled from block to block, I thought how I would have given up ever setting my feet on a deck if it would have stopped this from happening. I wished we lived above that buffer zone between the good and the bad, and I wished the biggest problem in my life right now was choosing what university I would attend after high school. It wasn't that way, though, and my brother was in trouble. I had a creeping feeling it was more trouble than I could deal with.

A bit away from the park, I kicked my board up and skirted around the block, coming to the place where Indy had been dealing. I found a corner hidden in shadow and sat, watching.

It only took ten minutes for a car to idle up to the curb and a figure to come out from the darkness, and as I peered, I recognized Indy's shape. I stood, walking across the street as the car pulled away. Indy saw me and stopped. I walked up to him. "Hi."

He looked at his feet. "Hi."

"I'm sorry about last night. I was mad."

Indy looked over his shoulder, nervous. "You should really go, Tate."

"Have the police talked to you yet?"

He shook his head. "No. But you've got to go, Tate. Leave right now."

"They're bad people, Indy."

Indy looked over his shoulder again, and my eyes followed his glance. Will walked from the shadows, that smarmy grin on his face. "You just don't know when enough is enough, do you, Taterboy?" He didn't stop walking, and as he reached me, he threw a roundhouse punch and clocked me square on the ear. I spun to the side, dizzy from the punch and my ears ringing, and came back around to face him.

And stared down the barrel of a pistol. He cocked the hammer back, the click echoing against the concrete pillars surrounding us, my heart stopping on a dime, all the pain in my head vanishing in a millisecond. He smiled, his eyes unflinching. "That was for the mistake you made, Taterboy. Now I'm going to tell you one more time. We've got business, and it doesn't include you. Got it?"

Indy's eyes grew wide with fear. "Will, come on, man. . . ."

Will chuckled. "It's all good, Indy. Your brother here just needs to learn his place, and it ain't here. No problems otherwise." He looked at me. "Isn't that right, Tate?"

I looked from Indy to Will. "The police are talking to everybody."

He smiled. "If I didn't know that, I suppose I'd be called stupid. But I'm not stupid, Tate, and I don't want you to be stupid, either." He glanced at Indy, and then his eyes flashed back to me. He grinned wickedly. "You understand what I'm saying?"

I looked at the black hole at the end of the barrel of that pistol, and it seemed to grow. My knees shook, and I knew all at once that if I pushed it with this guy, my brother and I would end up dead. "Yeah, I understand."

He didn't lower the gun. "Good. Now get the fuck out of here. And keep your mouth shut or I'll shut it for you."

I looked at Indy, wanting him to come with me, but he shook his head. I left then, my head hanging in shame, my knees shaking, and a sick feeling in me that I'd never felt before.

It was well after two in the morning when I got home, and when I kicked my board up at the sidewalk, I saw a figure sitting on the front porch. As I came near, I saw it was Mom.

She looked at me in the darkness. "Hi."

I sighed. "I suppose the front porch is becoming the meeting place."

"I want you to take me to him."

I shuffled, not knowing what to say. "I can't do that."

"Why? You know where he is."

"I do know. But I can't."

Her eyes searched me. "You don't know what to do, do you?"

I swallowed. "Not really."

She nodded, her eyes drifting back to the street. "Do you remember when you were little and we had that secret sign?" She held up her pinkie finger and wiggled it. "It meant that whatever you said or did was between you and me and nobody else, and that I wouldn't say anything to anybody unless you said it was okay."

I chuckled, remembering. "Yeah."

"I never told anybody anything, Tate," she said, looking at me and raising her finger. Tears glistened in her eyes. "Tell me."

I looked at her finger for a moment. "He's dealing drugs for a guy he knows. A bad guy. Serious bad guy."

She took a breath.

I put my hand on her knee. "I saw him tonight. He's fine. Just messed up about things."

She shook her head. "He's not fine, is he?"

I sighed. She always knew. "No. But he will be."

"I want you to take me to him."

I thought of Will. "I can't do that, Mom."

"Why?"

No matter what kind of weight the pinkie sign held, I knew that if I told her that Will carried a gun and had pulled it on me, she'd call the cops. I couldn't do that. They'd arrest Indy, and whatever chance he had of getting out of this without ruining his life would be gone. "I just can't."

She took my hand. "Tell me, Tate. Please. What's going on? I don't care if he's high or stoned or anything. I just want to talk with him."

I pulled my hand away. "Anything I'd say would be a lie, Mom, and I'm not going to lie to you. I'm sorry."

She looked at me. "Then I have no choice."

"What?"

"I'm calling the police and filing a missing-person report."

I lowered my head, staring at the concrete step. "Please, don't. You don't know . . ."

She stood. "That's exactly right, Tate. I don't know. But he's my son and he belongs here."

"If you tell them he's dealing, they'll nail him, Mom. And you pinkie-promised."

"Tell him I want to see him."

"I will. But I can't make it happen. Only he can."

She scratched the top of my head. "Okay, then."

"Are you going to tell Dad he's dealing?"

"No. Not now."

"Thanks."

She opened the screen door. "This has to come out, though. You know that. I can't hide something this serious from your father."

I stared at the street. "I know."

CHAPTER TWENTY-ONE

"In bed," I said, then glanced at my dad, who did not look like a happy man. Two detectives stood in our living room, one carrying a laptop case. My dad stood in front of them with his arms crossed, his posture threatening. My insides were still twisted up from Will's gun the night before, and my mind raced about what I should say.

"You were in bed the night of the murder." The skinny, balding one nodded, scribbling in a notebook. He looked up at me. "What about your brother?"

I glanced at Mom. "I don't know."

The other detective, pale, pudgy, and soft-spoken, studied our living room. He looked at my dad. "And you don't know where Indy is, Mr. Brooks?"

"No."

"Is there a family issue going on, sir?"

Dad didn't like the law, had no use for them, and pretty much thought they were a bunch of nosy, greedy bastards. "What goes on in this house is none of your business."

The detective nodded, unaffected by the statement. "We're trying to find a killer, sir."

Dad glared at him. "Then find a killer. My boys aren't involved with those kinds of people. My son was asked to leave our home due to a disagreement. If that's against the law, arrest me."

The skinny detective broke in. "Understandable, Mr. Brooks. If we could just have Tate look at a surveillance tape, we'll be out of your hair in no time."

Dad nodded, and the detective went to our living room table, unzipping his case and taking out the laptop. He moved his finger on the touch pad. "We believe this to be the beginning of the assault that ended with the victim's death. Please watch." He clicked the play button, and the video began just as Piper said it did. The scene was fuzzy, dark, and shadowed, and it was hard to see anything but two shapes, one with a stick or bat.

Halfway through, as one figure raised the stick, the detective stopped the video. "Do you recognize the figure with the weapon, Tate? Do his movements, his posture, anything at all, look familiar?"

"No."

The detective nodded, then clicked the zoom on the browser, capturing the upper left of the frame. "See that there?" He pointed to the corner. "That shape is a person. A witness. Or an accomplice."

Dad and I peered at the figure standing there. I looked close. The detective asked again, "Familiar at all, Tate? This is important, so please, look carefully."

I shook my head. "You can't even see."

"I know it's hard. This resolution is the highest we have available, but please look."

I did. After a moment, I sighed. I couldn't tell if it was Will or his uncle. "It could be anybody."

He clicked Play again and stayed zoomed in on the shape. It didn't move, just stood there as the other two figures went out of camera range. In another few seconds, he clicked Stop and closed the case. "You're sure?"

"Yeah. The crew doesn't night-skate that often, but tons of guys do."

"Your 'crew' would be Thomas 'Piper' Sandusky, Sid Valentino, your brother Indy, and yourself, correct?"

"Yes."

He zipped the case up, turning to my dad. "Mr. Brooks, it is important that we speak to Indy. If you see him, please contact us." He took a card from his wallet and handed it to him. "Anything at all will help. And if you'd like to file a report to find your son, we can help with that, too."

Dad brought himself up. "He can find my door on his own and make things better if he chooses." He glared at the detective. "Maybe you should do something about the scum in this city *before* this kind of thing happens."

The tension was palpable. The detective clenched his teeth. "We do what we can with the manpower we have, sir. We arrest them, the courts let them out. Just doing our jobs."

"Line 'em up beside the damn judges and shoot 'em all."

That got a laugh from both detectives. I pictured my dad shooting his son in that line. Dad loosened up a bit, then held his hand out. They shook. "I hope you catch him. And if Indy comes home, I'll contact you."

"Thank you," the skinny one said, then turned to me. "Tate, if anything comes to mind at all about that tape, call."

After the detectives left, my dad faced me. "I don't want you down there anymore."

I shrugged. "It's not that bad. We stay away from that side of the park."

"Where is Indy?"

Even though I was telling him the truth as far as I knew it, I knew this question would come up. I hated lying. Every time I did, things just went from bad to worse because I sucked at it. I glanced at Mom, hoping she'd keep her promise. "I don't know."

"Don't lie to me."

Mom cut in. "He's not, Dan. Tate and I talked last night. He doesn't know where he's staying."

He furrowed his brow. "Well, what the hell is going on, then?" He looked at me. "Why the detectives, Tate? Why did they come to our house?"

"They're questioning everybody who skates down there. I swear, Dad, I have no idea what happened to Lucius or who did it. They even talked to Pipe and Sid. Nobody knows."

"This doesn't add up, son."

I wished right then, more than ever, that I could trust my dad, but I couldn't. I wanted to tell him about Will, the gun,

Indy dealing, and everything, but I couldn't. He wasn't like Mom. He'd railroad it just like he railroaded everything. Just bull his way through and do it his way. "I don't know. Sorry."

Dad looked at Mom, then turned to me. True concern and worry etched his face, and I was surprised. I don't think I'd ever seen my father afraid, but I could tell he was. He cleared his throat. "You tell Indy to come home. No more yelling, no more trouble. Just come home. I'll stay out of his way, Mom can be the one to talk with him, and that's it. You'll tell him that?"

"Yeah, I will. I promise."

CHAPTER TWENTY-TWO

The entire skater population at school buzzed with gossip. Who was the dude? Skaters usually weren't on the top of the list as far as spreading gossip and rumors was concerned, but when you had the cops interviewing dozens of guys, it made some waves.

Sid and Piper caught up with me at the wall during lunch, and Sid, of course, brought it up. "Duuuude, I'm putting some pieces together that don't make a pretty puzzle."

I sighed. "What are you now, a detective or something?"

"No, but Lucius dead plus Will taking over his territory equals trouble in one way or another for Indy. The cops will find out."

I shrugged, thinking about what Piper had said, which was exactly the same thing. "I don't know."

Sid snorted, spitting a loogie. "Common sense says the guys in that video are Will and his uncle."

"Yeah," I said.

He stuck his hands in his pockets. "What are we going to do?"

I shrugged. "I don't know."

Piper cut in. "Have you talked to Indy?"

I shrugged again. "A little bit."

"What'd he have to say?"

"I just asked him to come home. He wouldn't."

Piper laughed. "You were always the worst liar in the world. I swear."

I clenched my teeth. "Will was with him when I did. He pulled a gun on me."

Piper's eyes widened. "No shit?"

"Yeah."

"Tate . . ."

"I know, Pipe, I know. I just about crapped my pants." I told them what Will had said, too, about staying away.

Sid grunted. "Bullets can make you dead. You know that, right?"

Piper lit a smoke. "He's, like, the hard-corest dude I've ever known, man."

I kicked my feet against the wall. "Have the police talked to him?"

Sid shrugged. "Only he knows that. The guy is like a ghost. Here, there, and everywhere, but nowhere you can find him."

"I know where he lives, and if I know, the cops do, too."

Piper took a bite of a Snickers bar, exhaling a lungful of smoke as he chewed. "Good. Maybe they're onto him."

I looked at my feet, torn up and confused. "I should have told them about it. About him and Indy dealing."

Piper shook his head. "And then what? You said Will threatened you about it. Besides, unless the cops are as stupid as they seem, they'll end up knowing who the new dealers are in the area. They can put two and two together just like we can."

I grunted. "Yeah, and that means they'll tie Indy in to things."

Piper shook his head again. "He was the last one I figured would get into this stuff, you know?"

Sid watched a drunk bum across the street stumble by. "Maybe we should do an intervention. Like they did on *The Sopranos*. We could tie him to a chair, and you could beat him up with a garden hose until he realizes how stupid he is."

"Great idea." Piper rolled his eyes. "Maybe you could ask your alien friends to abduct him and give him an anal probe. That might work, too."

"I don't have direct contact with them like that. Besides, they probe for genetic-mutation purposes."

I hopped down. "I'm heading home after school, guys. No park today."

Piper nodded. "I'm entering the Pro Skater Invitational. You?"

That was the least of my worries. "No."

He sighed. "Indy will be okay, Tate. Don't sweat it. They'll nail the dude who killed Lucius, they'll bust Will or something, and this will blow over."

"Yeah."

He pleaded with me, refusing to let the Invitational go. "At least enter. Then if things clear up, you can do it. If not, bail out and no sweat."

"We're not sponsored."

He smiled. "That's why we have to find one. Come on." He grimaced at Sid. "Sid will even compromise his rock-solid principles and do it. We could give 'em a run for their money, that's for sure, and if you can get Indy out of this shit and make him do it, we'll stomp all over Corey and his crew."

I didn't answer.

"At least think about it?"

"Okay."

Sid started humming "It's the End of the World as We Know It" by R.E.M. as I walked away. I had to smile at that one, even if the world did seem like it was ending.

CHAPTER TWENTY-THREE

Kimberly Lawson stood at the exit I usually take after school, and as I walked through the doors, she smiled and said hello. She hadn't been in class since I'd watched her volleyball game, and I was surprised she stood waiting. I smiled. "Been skipping class, huh?"

She laughed. "Sick." She paused, then said, "So, you noticed I was gone?"

Almost by accident, our eyes met for a moment. "I guess so."

She blushed. "That's nice."

I smiled. "Don't forget, I beat people up and rob them."

"And you go to volleyball games. I saw you there."

"Yeah. I was passing by and heard the noise."

She giggled. "Oh. I thought there was probably some girl you liked in there."

"Don't you have some sort of practice to go to, Miss Busybody?"

She smiled. "Yes. Orchestra prep. We have a concert tonight."

"You're in orchestra, too?"

She rolled her eyes. "Violin. First chair. I hate it."

"Why do it, then?"

She shrugged, looking away. "Hungry?"

"I thought you had orchestra."

She giggled. "I do."

"But you want to get something to eat."

She nodded.

"With me."

"Yes."

I hesitated. "Okay. But you have to answer one question first."

"What?"

"Why."

She looked at me. "Why?"

"Yeah. Why do you want to go with me?"

She looked at her feet. "Because I thought about what you said. About following all the rules no matter what. That, and you came to my game."

"Why me, though? We're like salt and pepper."

"Because you're different. And you came to see me."

"I didn't come to see you."

She smiled again. "Yes, you did."

I sighed. "Okay, I did, but I was just walking by and decided to come in."

"I'm glad you came by." She looked down the street. "So, are you coming with me?"

"Sure. Where?"

She smiled and we began walking. "I loooove the chimichanga at Señor Froggy, but my parents don't believe in fast food."

I shrugged, not understanding. "What does that have to do with what you believe in?"

She laughed.

"What now?"

She was almost giddy. "Nothing."

"You just do whatever your parents say, don't you?"

She skipped once, her ponytail bouncing. "Yep."

I laughed. "Living dangerously, huh?"

"Yep."

• • •

We sat in the back corner of the joint while Kim chomped down on her second chimi and I finished a third burrito. We talked about school and volleyball and Indy, minus the drug-dealing thing, and the Skater Invitational coming up and some kind of leadership summer camp that she'd just signed up for. All in all, it was sort of cool to talk to somebody about my bro and my family, and it just seemed to come out easy. I even told her about "Stealing Home" and me trying to give it to his English teacher.

She popped a Mexi-nugget in her mouth, then sat back and rubbed her stomach. "Ahhhh. I am SO full."

"So you really can't eat fast food?"

She nodded. "They're all into the natural-food thing. No chemicals and stuff. If I ever have any time, I can sneak away, but not often."

"What do you do? I mean, your schedule?"

She counted off on her fingers. "Volleyball four days a week and Saturdays, track during track season, violin lessons three times a week, cheerleading when I have time, babysit my cousins twice a week at night, homework, church, camp during summer." She rolled her eyes. "It never ends."

I smiled. "The perfect angel and her perfect family."

She looked at me for a moment, then burst out laughing, looking down at her tray.

I decided she was psycho. "What's so funny?"

"Perfect, huh? You have no idea."

I shrugged. "Sounds perfect to me."

"It's not."

"How, then?"

She stopped laughing. "You really want to hear it? You really want to hear how not-perfect my perfect family is?"

"Sure."

"You know when we saw you in the church parking lot that night?" Her eyes glinted. "When you were beating up and robbing Corey?"

I nodded.

"We weren't going to church. We were going to family counseling. I didn't mention that in my schedule." She popped a potato ball in her mouth. "My dad goes Tuesdays, my mom Wednesdays, and we all go Mondays and Saturdays."

"Why?"

"Well, the perfect family isn't so perfect. On the outside we are, because that's all that counts, right? All about the look, huh?"

"What are you saying?"

"I'm saying that my mom found out eight months ago that my dad has been cheating on her for the last twelve years, she's hooked on Xanax because of it, my sister wets her bed every night because they fight constantly, I hate them both, and the only thing they can tell me is that I'll end up being a nothing unless I keep doing what I'm doing, which is being perfect." She grunted—it was half a laugh and half an expression of disgust. "I've got to turn out just like them, right?"

"That sucks."

She nodded with a sad, small smile. "No, it doesn't suck. It's a joke. We're a good churchgoing family, my mom volunteers at a hospice, my sister is a premier gymnast for her age, I'm almost a god, my dad is an upright family man with a great job, we have backyard barbecues, donate money to the church, bake cookies for charity events. And when everybody isn't looking, my dad screws his girlfriend, my sister pees her pants, and my mom pops pills."

I looked at her. "What do you do?"

She stopped smiling. "I do everything I'm supposed to because I don't know what else to do."

"Why not start living your life for yourself?"

She shrugged. "I'm here, aren't I?"

I smiled. "Yes, you are, but you're miserable."

"You're here, too, and"—her eyes glinted again—"I could say the same about you."

"You're talking about Indy?"

"Yes. And your dad."

"They're my family."

"Same as me."

I frowned. "So I should just blow them off and not care?"

"No. But you know what I think you should do?"

"What?"

"I think you should do the skate thing. I'd come to see it."

I looked out the window. "It's not the right time."

"You want to, though. And you're good. At least that's what everybody says."

I shrugged, somehow happy that she was interested enough to know that I was good. "It's just not the right time."

"I'll make you a deal, then."

"A deal?"

She nodded. "You do the Invitational and I'll quit orchestra."

I looked at her, thinking about it. "Serious?"

"Yes."

I thought about Indy and all the crap that was going on, then thought about skating in the arena. I'd have to practice big-time. Excitement rippled through me. Maybe I could do it. Maybe it was time to look after myself for once. "Deal."

She held out her hand, and we shook. "Deal," she said.

As we walked out the door, she stopped. "You know what I think you should do also?"

"What?"

"I think you should take that story Indy wrote and make her read it. The Greater Spokane Area Young Writers Competition is taking entries, and if it's as good as you say it is, you should enter it. The only thing is that since the schools sponsor it, it has to be recommended by a teacher."

"A competition?"

She nodded. "I entered mine already."

"You like writing?"

"No, but my honors teacher insisted."

I laughed. "Is there anything you're not great at?"

She smiled, and that sad flicker came to the corners of her mouth. "Yeah. Being myself. See ya, and thanks. I had a great time."

I said goodbye, tempted to kiss her, but I didn't. I liked Psycho Girl. I don't know why, but I did. Maybe it was because she was totally different than what she seemed.

CHAPTER TWENTY-FOUR

Kim and I had lunch the next day—7-Eleven nachos that were just about the grossest thing on the planet—and we talked some more. She'd told her parents she was quitting orchestra, and World War III had broken out, but she'd held her ground. Well, not exactly, she explained. She'd locked herself in the bathroom for three hours while her mom railed on her through the door. I smiled, visualizing Kim crouched up in the tub yelling at her mom to go away.

I looked at her, surprised at first, but not on second thought. I guess that no matter what people look like, we all have the same feelings. Just different shells protecting us from who we really are.

As we walked back to campus, I took her hand in mine. "We all have our crap, huh?" I said.

She swung our hands between us, then laughed. "I guess we do."

We walked half a block in silence after that, and I couldn't help myself any longer. "I'm not very good at this."

"This what?"

I looked ahead at the campus. "Liking you."

She laughed, squeezing my hand. "Is it hard for you to like people, Mr. Tough Guy?" she said.

I laughed, thinking of Ms. Potter. "Well, yeah, it is."

When school got out, I skated to Under the Bridge. Sid and Pipe were nowhere to be found, so I sat on the concrete wall as late students filtered across the grounds. I unzipped my pack and took out "Stealing Home," staring at the title page. Indy's English teacher came to mind. What a crack. She'd never accept it.

I looked up, staring across the street at a bum wheeling a shopping cart down the sidewalk. He wore camos, patent leather dress shoes, an old turquoise sweatshirt, and a baseball cap. His cart was loaded with all his stuff, and I wondered what he'd been like before he'd become a living throwaway. Maybe his coach screwed him, too.

I shook my head. There had to be a way to get Indy away from Will. Frustrated, I stuffed "Stealing Home" in my pack and headed across the street to the school. I had to try again, but couldn't bring myself to deal with his bitch of a teacher.

Mr. Halvorson—the teacher who had thrown Indy up against the locker for skating down the hall—sat behind his desk, the empty chairs in his classroom almost cold now that the butts of twenty-eight Honors English seniors were no longer in them. He didn't like Indy. I couldn't think of a teacher who did, though.

He looked up when I came in. "Can I help you?"

I looked at the foot of his desk. A baseball bag, cleats sticking out the open top, lay there. "I'm Tate Brooks. We met the other day."

He nodded, indifferent. "Yes. Your brother Indy. The skater."

I nodded. "The person."

He sat back, crossing his ankle over his knee. "What can I do for you, Mr. Brooks?"

I shifted on my feet. "I was wondering if you could read something."

He pursed his lips. "You're a writer?"

I shrugged. "I was just hoping you could take a look. Maybe let me know what you think."

He contemplated. "Why not give it to your English teacher?"

I balked, digging for an answer. My teacher would know in a heartbeat that I hadn't written "Stealing Home." I shrugged again. "I heard you had a book published, so I was figuring you'd be the best judge." I smiled. "That and you're the department head."

He smiled, taking the compliments as intended. "What is it?"

I dug in my pack, taking out "Stealing Home" and handing it to him. "It's not very long. Just a short one."

He studied it. "'Stealing Home,' huh?" He grinned. "A baseball story?" .

"Yeah." I played dumb, pointing to his baseball bag. "You're the coach?"

He nodded. "I guess you could say by default. I'm the only faculty member with college ball under his belt, so I was nominated. We lost Coach Xavier two years ago to the University of Arizona."

"Cool."

Mr. Halvorson tucked the story in his satchel. "Depends on who you talk to, huh?" He stood. "I'll get to it as soon as I can."

I smiled. "Thanks. I appreciate it."

• • •

I stared at the blackness of the ceiling for over an hour, my mind running over all the things that could solve our issues, and anger bubbled up in me. I was used to dealing with things head-on. Have a problem, either bust your knuckles on it or blow it off. This was different.

The barrel of that pistol aimed at my face scared me more than I liked to admit. And the flashing image of Will with his finger on the trigger and that cold look in his dark eyes, telling me he'd like to pull it, shook me to the bone. Fistfights were one thing, but staring at your death was over the edge for me.

I'd always known what to do. Even if I didn't think about all the different angles of something like my mom or Indy did, and even though I used my fists instead of my mouth more than I should, I'd always trusted my instincts to deal with what was right and wrong. Now I realized the barrel of that pistol was forcing me to think, because I was afraid. I hated being afraid, but I had to figure this out, and I had to figure it out before Indy got in too deep.

I had to get to him. Talk to him. Find out the whole story. Tell him Mom wanted to see him, and that Dad would lay off him if he came home. I rose from bed and dressed in the dark, slipping my shoes on and opening the window. Throwing my board onto the lawn, I crawled out, and the night met me with as much foreboding as I met it with.

There were two places I knew Indy might be, and I ran a pretty good chance of coming across Will at either. Will and his damn gun. Will and those cold eyes. With a shudder, I realized he was the first person I'd ever *really* been scared of. A person who rubbed me so the wrong way that I wanted nothing to do with him ever again. I realized what it was then. Will didn't care. I did. And my dad had always said that if you've got nothing to lose, you'll do anything to win.

I just wanted out of this situation because my dad was right. I couldn't win. But I couldn't get out, either. I couldn't give up on my brother.

Fifteen minutes later, I was across the street and in the shadows Under the Bridge, waiting to see Indy come out of his hidey-hole to peddle drugs. I waited. Must be a slow night. No cars, no sign of movement. Then a car rounded the corner and idled down the street.

They stopped at the curb, waiting, and a figure came out of the shadows a moment later. I could tell right away it wasn't Indy. The figure was much bigger, tall, skinny, and slope-shouldered. Not Will. Somebody else. Probably some kid they'd sucked in just like Indy.

I waited around for a half hour and four cars more, but the same guy came out each time, so I split, skating further downtown to the Coldstone. I couldn't knock on the door, I knew that, but I figured if I hung out long enough, he might come out or go in. Not much of a chance, but the only alternative was to lie in bed all night staring at the ceiling.

As I skated, I thought about Mindy, the prostitute I'd talked with, and wondered if she'd be there. I wondered if everybody down there had a story like hers, sad and screwed up and full of all the things nobody wanted to hear about in a world painted with just the right tones. I sighed, kicking my board up as I reached the corner of the building.

And almost ran into Will. I stepped back, my breath catching at the surprise. He smiled, the streetlight over us casting a glowing bubble on the dirty sidewalk. "Well, if it's not Tatertot."

I gripped my board, not wanting this. "Where is he?"

He shrugged, grinning wider. "Not here. But I am." He walked closer, facing me. "You want to settle our little problem, skater boy? Your bro isn't here to see what I'm going to do to you."

I met his eyes, and everything I'd seen in them before was there now, but just bare and raw. Nothing to lose. "I don't have a problem with you, Will. I just want to know where he is."

He shook his head, his teeth flashing. "You don't seem to

get it, Tater. Your brother is finished being second dog to you."
A wicked look came across his face, and he nodded, enjoying
this game he was playing.

"I'm not top dog to him."

"You're right." He leveled his eyes at me. "I am."

The gun I knew he had on him loomed huge in my head.
"I don't give a crap about what you do or anything, Will, and
we don't have a problem. He doesn't belong here. That's all.
I've got nothing against you."

"Oh, he belongs here, all right. It's you who doesn't, and
maybe we should settle that score right now, because I've got
something against you."

"I don't want to fight you."

He laughed. "It ain't going to be a fight, you stupid fuck."

I shook my head, my heart hammering. I could feel it
coming. "Stay away from him, Will. It's not worth it. You can
pick anybody else. Just not him."

He smiled, reaching behind his back. "You don't have shit
to say about—"

I hit him with the flat of my board square on the side of
the face, and he went down like a lump, crumpling to the
sidewalk, his cheek split open, deep and bleeding. He moaned,
and before he knew what was going on, I reached down and
fumbled at his waist, bringing out a snub-nosed revolver and
stuffing it in my pocket. In an instant I knew I was so far in
this that there was only one way out.

I should kill him. I should put the barrel of the pistol to
his head and pull the trigger. I should end it the only way it

would truly end, because if I didn't do it, he'd end up doing me. I took the pistol out of my pocket. He opened his eyes. I put the barrel to his forehead. I cocked the hammer back.

But I couldn't. I wouldn't. I wouldn't be him. I was more. Better. Kim watching me beat that jackhole up in the parking lot flashed through my mind. No. I would be better. But I could scare him. I bent close to his ear. "You don't care, Will. I know that. And I was afraid of it. But I'm not anymore. You picked the wrong family. The wrong kid. Leave him alone." Then I was gone, walking down the sidewalk with my bloodied board in my hand, my knees shaking and a pistol in my pocket.

And I knew I was in trouble.

CHAPTER TWENTY-FIVE

Every bone in my body screamed to hand the pistol over to my dad the next morning, but I didn't. He'd flip out, pry the truth out of me, and go on a rampage, and I didn't want that. My dad might be a tough son of a bitch, but he couldn't stop a bullet. Neither could I, though, and my mind was blank about what to do.

There was no way I could give it to Mom, either. I knew her well enough that I knew the first thing she'd do would be the right thing. She'd call the police. I thought again about Ms. Potter. It's not the rules you follow, it's how you follow the rules. Right isn't always right, and for Indy's sake, I had to figure this out before I spilled the beans.

I stuffed it in my pack before I left for school. Dad didn't say a word when I left, and Mom was already in the salon for one of her early birds. No sweat off my back. I didn't feel like talking anyway. I felt like dissolving into nothing. Just like Sid had after Cutter died.

I knew Angie and her friends hung out in the student parking lot under the freeway before school, and that was where I went. She wasn't there, but three of her friends were. I'd gone to junior high with one of the guys, Pauly Higgins, and we'd gotten along well enough. He'd skated until he got into the Goth scene, and we'd drifted apart. The guy was as demented as he looked, but cool, and he always wore the long black overcoat, chains, makeup, and dyed black hair that made them who they were. "Hey, Paul."

He nodded, his eyes heavy with black eyeliner. "'Sup, Tate."

"Looking for Angie."

He laughed, shaking his head. "She doesn't come around much anymore."

"Where does she live?"

"Thirteenth and Bernard. Green-and-white house on the corner." He eyed me. "Looking for your brother?"

I nodded. Word spread quickly.

"I've seen him."

"Where?"

"Rave down on Second last night. You know the warehouse?"

"Yeah."

"There's one there almost every night now." He shook his head, pausing. "He's hanging with that skinhead, you know." He eyed me. "The skinhead has his tag on Angie, so be careful."

"Yeah."

167

He stared at me, the black eyeliner making the almond-shaped orbs look ominous. "Guy is bad news."

I nodded.

He stepped away from his friends, motioning me away. We walked, and he lit a smoke. "Listen, Tate, I'm not the one to be telling you this because I like my dope as much as the next guy, but I always liked you." He exhaled. "Your bro is dealing heavy at the raves. Not the light shit, either."

"I know."

He nodded. "Knew it wasn't your crew's bag. Thought I'd let you know."

"Thanks."

"No sweat, Tate. Indy was always cool."

As I turned away, he called to me again. I looked at him. "Yeah?"

Pauly frowned. "He's using, too."

• • •

Piper sat on the grass near the east entrance to the school when I got there, and I gave him some skin. We had a few minutes before class started. "What's up?"

He shook his head. "Old man went on a binge last night, dude. I swear when that guy starts on the booze, the world is going to pay."

Piper's dad was the worst kind of drunk. "You sleep in the garage again?"

He nodded. "Yeah. Had to padlock the damn door from

the inside this time. He was falling all over himself banging on it." He paused. Piper's dad wasn't a topic he spoke of often. "Indy back at school today?"

I shrugged. *He's using.* "I don't know if they'll even let him back in now."

Piper smiled. "Funny thing. I saw Will this morning hanging around the park. Like he was looking for somebody or something."

I shrugged again. "Huh."

Piper studied me. "Looked like a truck hit the side of his face."

"Wow."

"You wouldn't know anything about that, huh?"

"Yeah."

He deflated, slumping his shoulders. "Crap, Tate."

I looked off, down Under the Bridge. "Tell me something I don't know, Piper."

"How'd it happen?"

I told him, adding what I'd seen in the apartment.

He grunted. "The gun."

I nodded.

"Not your run-of-the-mill scum, huh?"

I shook my head. "I don't think so."

He narrowed his eyes. "What'd you do with the gun?"

"I have it."

His eyebrows popped up. "With you? Like, here?"

I nodded.

He looked around. "Not a good situation."

"I couldn't leave it home. I know Mom searches our room, and *Playboys* and grass are different than a pistol."

"Dude, bringing a gun to school is, like, a capital offense now. They'll fry you."

I shrugged. "If I threw it away, a kid could find it."

Piper looked at me. "You're going to do something stupid, aren't you?"

I shrugged again. We'd known each other too long. "I'm not going to do anything unless Will does. I never wanted a problem in the first place."

"Listen, Tater, you know I hate Big Brother as much as the next normal-thinking person, but maybe you should think about going to the detectives. If he can get one gun, he can get another."

"Yeah, then they'll bust Indy for dealing, and you know that if Will or his uncle did kill that dude, they'll come after me for snitching them out. No way. This is street, and you should know that."

He stood. "I think you should go to the pigs."

"You going to say anything?"

He shook his head. "No, but I think you should."

• • •

By third period the gun in my pack felt like it weighed a thousand pounds, and I'd been looking over my shoulder every five seconds in the halls. *Jumpy* wasn't the word, and I spent the whole hour wondering what I should do with it.

When class let out for lunch, I walked to the student office. The lady behind the counter didn't look up. I cleared my
throat. A paper taped on the counter read YOUR MISTAKE IS
NOT MY PROBLEM. She kept her eyes down, writing in a ledger. "Yes?"

"Is Ms. Potter available?"

She looked up, irritated at the interruption, then frowned.
"Did you have a teacher's note or an appointment?"

"Uh, no. But it's sort of important."

"She's busy. You'll have to make an appointment."

"Ma'am, it's really sort of important that I see her—"

"I said you'll need to make an appointment. Ms. Potter
isn't on call for every student who wants to see her." She went
back to writing in her ledger.

I sighed. It was like every school in the world hired people
who considered anybody under twenty years old to be some
sort of subhuman organism. "She's a counselor."

"And . . . ?"

"Well, her job is to see students who want to see her.
That's what a counselor does."

She looked up, thin-lipped and irritated that I was inter-
rupting her job, which apparently was being the most miserable old lady in the world. "Make . . . an . . . appointment," she
said before looking down at her papers.

Something in me popped, and I didn't know whether to
laugh or scream my head off. I was trying to do the right
thing, but of course you can't do the right thing unless you do
it the right way. I tapped the counter. She looked up. I stared

at her. "Screw . . . you," I said, then walked to Ms. Potter's door and went inside.

She looked up when I came in. "Tate?"

I set my bag down, plopping in a chair across from her. "Yeah, I know. I don't have an appointment. Ms. Tightass out there let me know."

She groaned. "Not another f-bomb, I hope?"

"Nothing she didn't need."

Just then, her phone rang, and I could hear the lady out in the office squawking into the receiver. Ms. Potter smirked, then sighed. "I'll deal with it, Irene. Thank you. It won't happen again." Then she hung up, looking at me. "Tate, there's only so much I can do to help you. You have to help yourself, and doing these things doesn't help."

I shrugged. "Yeah, I know. As long as I do it your way, we're all good, right?"

She blinked. "What does that mean?"

I looked around, not interested in discussing why this sucked so much. "So, when we're talking, is there some sort of confidentiality thing that says you can't tell other people what we talk about?"

She eyed me. "Yes. Everything you say to me is confidential. Unless I believe you or another person is in danger, being abused, or otherwise being harmed. Or if you tell me that a crime has occurred."

"So basically, we should talk about the weather," I said, laughing with contempt.

She studied me. "What's going on?"

I looked at her. "I'm pissed, that's what's going on." I shook my head. "I've got a huge problem and I don't know what to do, and honestly, I'm in over my head, because I don't have anywhere to go."

She nodded. "And that makes you mad. I can understand that."

"No, you don't understand anything. You make me mad. This school makes me mad, because you're full of shit."

"Why?"

I frowned. "Your entire job supposedly exists to help us, but you set the whole system up to nail us, and it's bullshit." I clenched my teeth. "Unless you have some kid who needs a schedule change or lost a fucking library book, you're useless."

She swallowed, then cleared her throat. "What happened, Tate? Tell me."

I shook my head. "You expect me to tell you anything? You're here for this *school*, not the people in it. Just like that crack in the office."

She was flustered, and I almost felt bad for her. But it was the truth. I had a gun in my backpack, and I knew what would happen if I gave it to her, because according to this school, doing the right thing was the wrong thing. She looked at her desk, contemplating something I didn't know. "Tate, that's not true."

I smiled, sitting back in the chair. "I can prove it is true."

She looked at me. "Okay. Tell me."

"Okay, then. Let's just say there was this student. You knew him well enough, and you knew he was going through some crap. Sort of an on-the-edge kid who's trying to do things right. Well, one day this kid, he comes into your office. He's pretty shaken up, and he doesn't know what to do because some bad stuff happened. So you ask him what's wrong. He tells you a banger has been hassling him pretty bad. Turns out the banger pulls a gun on the kid, and the kid gets the gun away from him. Now, the kid can't give it to his parents or the police because of other stuff, but he knows the right thing to do is get it safe, you know? He doesn't want to dump it because somebody might find it and hurt somebody, right? So he comes in your office, tells you the story that he found it and wants to do the right thing by turning it over." I looked at her. "What would you do if that happened, Ms. Potter?"

A long silence passed. Then she spoke. "Well, I would have to call the police."

I nodded. "I know that. But what would happen to the kid for doing the right thing?"

She pursed her lips. "He would be arrested and charged with being in possession of a weapon and bringing it onto school grounds."

"And expelled, right?"

She swallowed, nodding. "He would be expelled."

I stood, grabbing my pack. "You told me there's always different ways to do things right, Ms. Potter. You're a liar. There's only your way, and that's not right," I said, stepping to the door. "See ya."

She looked at my pack. "There are other ways," she said quickly.

I looked at her.

She cleared her throat, then grabbed her purse. "Would you like to take a walk with me, Tate? Off school grounds?"

I studied her, wondering if she'd gone insane. "Sure."

So we walked. We walked through the halls and out a side door. She said nothing, but she was breathing heavier than our little stroll would dictate. I could tell she was nervous as we hit the sidewalk. We waited at the corner signal for a moment, standing as traffic passed, and then walked across the street when the light turned green. I smiled. "Nice weather, huh?"

She let out a stuttering laugh, gesturing to a bus-stop bench. "Let's sit."

We did.

She put her hands on her thighs. "We're off school grounds. I have no knowledge of what is in your backpack, I have not seen a weapon on school grounds, and you have not told me you are in possession of one."

"Yep."

"If you were to tell me that you found a weapon and would like to give it to me to turn in, that's your choice. But as we're not on school grounds, you would not be expelled."

"What, then?"

She bit her lip. "I would call the police, tell them I was in possession of a firearm that a student wanted to turn in, and sit here until they arrived to take it. I would hope the student would stay with me. I'm sure the police, seeing his intentions, wouldn't charge him with anything. They would question him and most likely contact his parents."

"You could lose your job for this."

"Actually, no, I couldn't. I would report what happened factually. I haven't seen a firearm on school property. A student needed to talk off school grounds, and it is my job to talk to students."

"Sid told me you were cool," I said.

"How is he?"

"Fine." I looked at her. "Are you nervous?"

"Yes. Very. I would appreciate it if you didn't touch your backpack."

I nodded. "Call the police, Ms. Potter."

• • •

Forty minutes and a ride in a cop car later, I sat staring at the wall of an interrogation room at the police department. All this over a stinking gun I wanted to turn in. Ms. Potter waited outside, after insisting that she give a statement to the detective in my support. That in itself surprised me again. She was going to bat for me, and I didn't really know how to take it.

A few minutes later, I groaned. As the door opened, the skinny detective who'd visited the house about the murder walked in. My dad followed him, his work clothes still covered in soot from his welding job. Mom followed him. Neither looked happy.

The detective sat across the table from me, motioning for my parents to take a seat next to me. Dad refused, standing with his arms crossed. My mother sat. I assumed everything was being recorded, because the cop introduced himself formally as Detective Larry Connelly of the Spokane Police Department. He opened a notebook, took the cap from a pen, then looked at me. "Please state your name."

I began, but my dad cut in. "Close your mouth."

Detective Connelly looked at my dad. "We need a statement, Mr. Brooks."

My dad's face was a rock. He kept his eyes on me. "Did you give a statement to the officer who brought you in, son?"

I nodded. "Yes."

"Was it the truth?" he said.

"Yes."

He looked at Detective Connelly. "You got your statement, and unless you tell me right now that the purpose of this little talk isn't to charge my son with anything, I want a lawyer."

The detective dropped his pen on the notebook, frustrated. "I can't promise anything, Mr. Brooks, but I can tell you that as of now, I am simply following up on a firearm-related incident concerning your son turning in a weapon to his counselor. I have no reason to believe your son gave a false report."

My dad took a moment, his eyes searching mine, and then he looked at Mom. She nodded, clearing her throat. "Go ahead, Detective."

The detective picked up his pen, then scanned the street cop's report. "Tate, you didn't name the person you acquired the pistol from. Who was it?"

"I didn't acquire it. I took it from him so he wouldn't shoot me."

He nodded. "Okay. Who was this individual?"

"A guy."

"And his name?"

I had to play this straight. If they knew Will was involved, they'd know Indy was, too. "He didn't show me his birth certificate."

Detective Connelly clenched his teeth, his jaw muscles working. "This isn't a game, Tate. It's serious."

"I know. That's why I gave the gun to my counselor."

He nodded again. "And that's great. But I need to track down who had the gun. You say in your statement that you had a conflict with a person, they pulled a gun on you, and you took it from him. I need more than that."

I shrugged. "That's what happened."

"And you won't tell me anything more?" he asked.

"Why should I? Doing the right thing might help you, but it only gets me fucked on the street."

Silence. The detective studied my face. Another moment passed. Then he spoke to my mom. "Mrs. Brooks, I believe that what occurred with your son Tate has to do with the murder of Lucius Singleton. I believe that your son knows more about the incident than he told me the night I visited your home. I believe your other son is involved somehow, too."

My insides shriveled, and I wondered what was going on. I glanced at my dad, then back to the detective. "I don't know anything more than you do. I swear. A guy had a beef with me, he pulled a gun, I took it from him. End of story."

Detective Connelly wrote something in his notebook. "Do you know an individual by the name of William Bradford?"

I didn't know a William Bradford. "No."

He smirked. "Otherwise known as 'Will,' who happens to be a friend of your brother, Indy."

I swallowed. "Yeah, I know him."

"And he's a drug dealer?"

My mind raced. If I pegged Will as the guy I got the gun from, it would put Indy in a bad situation. And me, too. "I've never seen him deal drugs."

"Have you heard that he deals?"

"You think Will killed Lucius?" I said, cutting to the chase.

"I don't know who killed him," Detective Connelly said.

"Me neither. And I'm not lying. I don't know anything about Lucius."

"What have you heard about it, then?"

"Probably the same as you. You brought Will's name up."

He looked at me. "Who did you get the gun from?"

I frowned. "Who do you think I got the gun from?"

"I think you got the gun from William Bradford. You and he have had problems, right?"

"We've had our differences."

"And you're not going to tell me you took the gun from him, are you?" the detective said.

I shook my head. I wasn't going to snitch out Will until I talked to Indy, but I ached to. "You seem to have all the answers. I guess you can take it from there."

"You're not doing anybody favors here, Tate. I'm not here to burn you. Really. I just need to solve a murder."

My dad cut in. "My son turned in a weapon to the proper authorities. If he's broken the law, charge him. If not, we're leaving. End of story."

CHAPTER TWENTY-SIX

"You're going to tell me what's going on, or I'm going to beat it out of you."

I leaned my head against the seat of Dad's truck. Mom had taken the car, and Dad had insisted I ride home with him. "I don't know what's going on."

He slammed on the brakes, screeching to a halt. The car behind us honked. He ignored it. "Tell me, Tate."

"Dad, that's it! I wish I did know! I wish I could tell you, but I can't. I swear. I don't know anything about Lucius."

He looked at me. The car honked again, this time longer. "Did you take the gun from this Will guy?"

"Yes."

"Why didn't you say so?"

I sighed as more cars honked. "Will you please go? You're blocking traffic."

He gunned it, yanking the steering wheel and turning

into a parking lot. He took a breath, then cut the engine. "Tate, I trusted you in there. I trust you now. Why didn't you tell him who you got the gun from?"

A flash of anger, wicked and sharp, ran through me. "Because Indy is dealing dope for him."

Dad sat back, staring at the ceiling of the truck. "Fuck."

"Yeah, fuck. And I've got to get Indy out of it before it all comes apart, Dad. That's why. His entire future is on the line, not to mention his life."

"Great. Your brother is dealing dope."

"No, your son is," I snapped. "Are we done?"

He fired up the truck. "Where is he? Take me to him."

"I don't know."

"Tate . . ."

"I said I don't know! If I did, I'd get him! What the fuck do you think I've been doing, Dad?"

He hit the steering wheel with his hand. "This is out of control! Why didn't you tell me what was going on?"

"Why would I? Because you give a crap? God, Dad, what did you think would happen? You kicked him out." He stared at me. "You think he's just been hanging around being a good boy?"

"Don't, Tate. Stop it. I've tried—"

I cut him off. "No, I won't stop it. You haven't done anything! Nothing! He's in trouble, and a big part of it is because everything has to be *your* way! Always your way, Dad, and now he's fucked, so if you want to get pissed at anybody, get pissed at yourself," I said, then opened the door.

He stared at me. "Where are you going?"

I sneered. "Where do you think?" I grabbed my board and slammed the door shut. As I ran, I saw Dad throw the truck into gear and spin around, trying to follow me, but I cut into a space behind a gas station and hopped a fence.

CHAPTER TWENTY-SEVEN

Angie's house surprised me in that it was nice. Small, but not a white-trash dump like I expected. I walked up the trimmed and edged walk to the front door and rang the bell. Nobody answered, so I rang again, hoping somebody was home. A minute later the door opened and Angie stood there, her makeup smeared and hair mussed as she rubbed her eyes. "What?"

"Is Indy here?"

She smirked. "No."

"Where is he?"

"I don't know. Last I saw him, he was passed out on my bedroom floor. You woke me up, asshole."

I resisted the urge to slam her face inside out, because I needed help. "He was here?"

"Yeah."

"You guys went to a rave last night?"

She yawned, nodding.

I studied her face. "He's in trouble, Angie. You know it, too."

She stared at me. "Maybe with you he is."

"No. I'm talking about Will. And his uncle."

She moved to close the door.

I stopped her. "Tell me what's going on, Angie."

"Fuck you, Tate. It's none of your business. And you'd better watch out, because Will has this thing about you. It's called hate. And you don't want to mess with him."

I'd tried. Given it the good go, and it hadn't worked. In a flash I had her by her T-shirt, and I pushed her in the house. She tried to get away, but I yanked her to the floor, sitting on her stomach and pinioning her arms against the tile.

Her eyes met mine. "You going to rape me now? Go ahead. Get your rocks off before you die, because you don't know what you're dealing with."

I looked down into her eyes and saw something there I didn't want to see. Utter and complete fear. Because of me. Of what I was. My anger disappeared, replaced with a sick feeling in my stomach. "You know more than I do, Angie, and I have to help him. Please."

She shook her head, her hair splayed on the floor. "I don't know anything."

"Don't lie."

"I'm not. They don't tell me anything. Every time his uncle comes to the apartment, they kick me out."

"Did Will kill Lucius?"

"I don't know."

I breathed, still sick and disgusted, then got up. She stayed on the floor. I swallowed. "I'm sorry."

She looked up at me, her fear replaced with spite. "The mighty Tate Brooks is scared, isn't he? And you know what? You should be. You should be scared, Tate."

"You're scared, too, Angie. Aren't you? You had no idea what you were getting into with Will, huh?"

She sat up, and tears came to her eyes before she spoke. "Maybe, but there's not a lot I can do about it."

"Break up with him, then. Get out."

She laughed, wiping her nose. "You don't know Will."

"I need to find Indy. Help me, and I'll help you. We'll get you both out of this."

She looked at me, and there was something in her expression that did scare me. I could tell she was trapped in something that she didn't like and, most likely, didn't know how to get out of. "I don't know where he is now, but he parties almost every night at the warehouse on Second."

• • •

When I got home, Mom and Dad sat in the living room, staring at me as I walked in the door. Ten minutes into both of them launching everything at me in their arsenal of parental weaponry, I finally exploded, yelling at both of them. "For the thousandth time, I don't know where he is, I haven't seen him for five days, he's dealing drugs, I don't know about Lucius, I took Will's gun, and that's it! God, you want me to leave, too?"

My mom spoke. "We're actively working with the police to find him, Tate. This can't go on like this anymore."

"Did you tell them he's dealing?"

Dad shook his head. "We're not doing this to hurt him. We just need to find him."

"Good luck with that one. *I* can't even find him. Are we done? I have homework."

At eight that night, I was hopelessly trying to study for a math test when the doorbell rang. Dad answered and I heard his voice, along with someone talking about "your son." A minute later, Dad called me out.

Mr. Halvorson stood in our living room, apologizing for dropping in unexpectedly. He held Indy's story. "Hello, Tate."

"Hi." I stuffed my hands in my pockets.

Mom came in from the bathroom, smiling and shaking Mr. Halvorson's hand. She offered him a cup of coffee, which he declined, and he looked at her and Dad. "Mr. and Mrs. Brooks, your son came to my classroom and handed me this story." He held "Stealing Home" out to my dad, who took it. "Have you read it?"

Dad frowned. "No, but if there's anything in it that you found offensive—"

Mom interrupted. "No, I don't believe we have, Mr. Halvorson."

Mr. Halvorson went on. "Anyway, I told Tate I'd read it, and I have. In fact, I've read it four times. It's far and away the best-written piece of fiction from a student I've ever seen. The voice is strong and personal, the narrative flows in an incredibly true and natural manner, and quite frankly, it breaks out of all the stylistic bounds so commonly found today. Your son is a natural writer, Mr. and Mrs. Brooks, and incredibly gifted."

Mom blushed, and Dad furrowed his brow.

Mr. Halvorson nodded to Mom. "As I told Mr. Brooks before you came in the room, I'm the department head for English at Lewis and Clark, and also the senior honors teacher. I'd like to invite Tate to my class for the rest of the year. I would also, with your permission and Tate's, like to submit this story for the Greater Spokane Area Young Writers Competition. The deadline was yesterday, but I can get late approval." He paused, then said, "Over two thousand writers compete for a writing scholarship, and I think it would have a good chance of winning."

Mom was beaming, and Dad held the story, unmoved. I shifted, crossing my arms.

Dad looked at me. "Well, Tate, how about it?"

"I didn't write it."

Mr. Halvorson recoiled, confusion spreading across his face. He pointed to the story in my dad's hands. "You didn't write this?"

"No."

Mr. Halvorson looked from my mom to my dad, then back to me. "Who did?"

"My brother."

Anger cut Mr. Halvorson's mouth into a slit. "Why would you—"

"Because you wouldn't have read it if you knew who wrote it."

Mr. Halvorson paused. "I would have read it, Tate. You didn't have to lie."

"I didn't lie. I never said I wrote it in the first place. I just asked you to read it. Besides that, you don't like Indy. Nobody at school does." I gestured to our room. "He's got a whole computer full of stuff in there. That's what he does instead of studying."

He nodded. "I wish you would have given me a chance before assuming, Tate."

I glanced at my dad, giving him a wicked look. "My brother doesn't have any more chances, Mr. Halvorson."

He looked at Dad. "Why hasn't his English teacher seen this? Or any of his other writing?"

Dad's eyes flashed. "If he ever went to class, maybe she would have."

I cut in. "She did see it. I took it to her."

Mr. Halvorson looked at me, perplexed. "She read it?"

"She refused to."

He grimaced. "That should not have happened. I'm sorry."

I shrugged. "He wrote a regular assignment paper at the beginning of the year, and she wouldn't accept it because it was 'inflammatory and had foul language.' Same old story."

Dad took a breath. "Why wasn't I told about this? I didn't know he . . ."

I looked at him. "Why didn't you ask?"

Tears welled in Mom's eyes, and Dad looked like he was about to skin me alive.

Mr. Halvorson sighed, then nodded. "I'm sorry to intrude

on a family matter." He paused. "Indy will be coming back to school soon?"

Mom looked at Dad. He crossed his arms over his chest. "Indy isn't living with us." With that, the tears in my mom's eyes ran down her cheeks. She whispered an apology and left the room.

Mr. Halvorson looked at the story. "Well, the offer still stands for him to join my class, and I'd enjoy talking with him if he's willing. May I submit this to the competition, Mr. Brooks?"

Dad handed it to him, his face a rock. "Do what you choose with it."

CHAPTER TWENTY-EIGHT

At twelve-thirty that night I unlatched our window, slid it up, and hopped out, the cool night air prickling the hair on my arms. Three houses down from ours, I dropped my board and skated.

Night skating is one of the coolest things to do in the world. With everything still and quiet but for your wheels rolling on the pavement, it's like skating in a dream. The glow cast from streetlights and the emptiness of the city either freak you out or make you feel like the pavement and rails and sets were made just for you. I wished Indy was with me.

We'd snuck out a few times to carve the bowls Under the Bridge on midnight prowls. The clattering echo of our boards ratcheting under the open cavern of concrete, along with the occasional late-night traveler rolling on the freeway above, was peaceful. Under the Bridge would be ours on those nights, and those were the times having a bro was the best.

I skated downtown, past the school and the park and

further, until I reached Second Avenue. Five blocks west of the school and set in an old industrial-storage area, the warehouse sat brooding like a dark beast, its huge roll-up doors closed and locked and the upper-story office windows dark and foreboding.

I'd been to a rave here before, and the warehouse was the perfect place for it. No houses around, no businesses open late, litter and garbage strewn in the gutters and along the barbed-wire-topped fences, with the occasional bum wandering around collecting empty pop cans, meant hundreds of teenagers could listen to live music, get stoned and plastered, and stumble around puking without much hassle from anybody.

Down a narrow alley on the side of the building was a small door with a big guy standing to the side of it. Long dyed-black hair; leather jacket; black fatigues; combat boots; pierced nose, ears, and lip; and tattoos running up the sides of his neck told me he wasn't a guy to be messing with. As I neared, he crossed his arms over his chest and waited for me. I nodded. "Cover?"

"Seven." He held his hand out. "Any fighting and you're out permanently, plus you get to deal with me. Bring your own booze and drugs. There's no water in the toilets, so if you piss in them I'll make you drink it back out with a straw."

I dug in my pocket, took out a ten, and handed it to him. He stuffed it in his pocket. I waited for my change. It didn't come. "You owe me three."

He shook his head. "I'm not a bank. Go in or split."

"You know Indy Brooks?"

He stared at me. I took that as a sign that I should get out of his face, so I walked past him and went inside. A single bulb hanging in a hallway dimly lit the way to a small alcove at the end, where two Goths stood smoking at a steel door. The beat of heavy music came through the wall. Another kid, this one sitting Indian-style, his hair covering his face, rocked back and forth slowly, chanting something low and indecipherable. I looked at him, and one of his buddies laughed. "Does it every time he trips the acid, man." He dug in his pocket, taking out a Baggie. "Five bucks a tab. Good stuff."

Good was all in the eye of the beholder, I thought, glancing at the tripping kid on the floor. "No thanks," I said, and the Goths stepped aside for me. I pushed the door open, and the smell of pot mixed with sweat hit me. At the far side of the huge room, a screamo band blasted the amps, and at least a hundred people formed a pit center stage, moshing and stage diving while groups of people—from hard-core punks to Goths to straights out for a night of the other side of life—listened, talked, smoke, drank, and watched the band.

I walked through the crowd, looking for Indy before I found Paul Higgins. He and five guys sat in a circle in the far corner, old car seats and half-rotted couch cushions under them as they passed a bong around. He waved when he saw me, yelling over the music, "Tater! Duuuude!"

I nodded, sitting next to him. He slapped me on the shoulder, calling for the bong and yelling, "Bring it over, guys. This is Tater. Old skater buddy. Best in the whole fucking city if you ask me."

I waved the bong away, looking around. "Busy place."

He nodded, leaning to my ear. The band raged. "Not even. You should see this shithole on Saturday nights. Packed with the dregs." He laughed, cackling at his stoned joke.

I sat back, listening to the band and glancing through the crowd. "Seen my bro?" I yelled to him.

He shook his head, taking a hit from the bong. He held his breath, then exhaled. "He usually doesn't hang on the floor."

I glanced at my watch, pushing the light button in the dimness. One-fifteen. "Where, then?"

He waved behind him, to a hallway. "There's five or six offices down there. No-man's-land. The hard-core hang there."

I studied the dark entryway littered with garbage, then stood, leaning down to Paul's ear. "Thanks, Paul. I owe you."

He smiled, shaking his head. "Just get him the fuck out, dude. He doesn't belong in there."

As I made my way through the crowd and walked down the hall, the music faded, and it took a minute for my eyes to adjust to the deeper shadows. I came to the first door, which stood open. Complete darkness greeted me, so I kept going. After three more empty rooms, I came to a closed door. Light flickered from beneath it. I put my hand on the doorknob, taking a breath and tensing. Will might be with him, and it would mean a fight. A big one. I wished I'd kept the gun, but it was too late for wishes.

I turned the handle and opened the door. At least a dozen people sitting and lying on ratty sofas, beanbags, lawn chairs, and old recliners dotted the room, all high or zoned out and talking in low murmurs. A cloud of smoke encapsulated my head—weed mixed with a toxic, harsh smell. Several people looked up, giving me indifferent stares before going back to talking. The tang of burned meth stung my nose.

A card table with a broken leg taped together stood in the center of the room, a half dozen lit candles on it, and bottles, cans, and garbage lay scattered between the groups of people. Two dim forms, a guy with a shaved and bristly head and his girl, lay on a mattress in the corner having slow-motion sex under a blanket, and I had to peel my eyes from them. From the look of disinterest everybody else had about it, I figured privacy wasn't too important when you were trashed out of your mind.

I scanned the room for Indy, peering through the shadows and the smoke at each guy until I came back to the couple on the mattress. Then I did a double take. I clenched my teeth as I walked across the room, standing above them. "Get up."

He turned his shaved head from the girl's neck, saw me, and smiled. "Hey, bro, what brings you to this domain?"

"Get up. Now."

The girl looked up at me with glazed eyes, then smiled, pulling Indy back to her. He giggled into her neck, then gave me an "I dare you" look. I reached down, grabbing his arm and yanking him up. "I said get up, man." I looked around, picked up his shirt next to the mattress, and threw it at him as he pulled his pants up.

Once buckled, he picked up his shirt, a grimace on his face. "Dude, just get the fuck out of here. Leave me alone."

"No."

He shook his head and plopped down on the mattress. "I'm not going anywhere."

Just then, one of the guys in the room spoke. He couldn't stop moving his hands, the meth stringing him out like a live wire. "You heard him, chief. Get out."

I ignored him, even as the rage in me built. "Put your shirt on, Indy."

The guy piped up again. "Hey, man, nobody tells anybody what to do around here. It's all cool."

I turned on him. I clenched my teeth. "You want your face caved in, *chief*?" I waited a moment, staring him down, and when he opened his mouth again, I jacked him in the face. He sprawled back, then lay still, moaning. Nobody moved. Nobody said a word. The candles flickered. Then I turned back to Indy, yanked him up, and dragged him out. He didn't fight me.

I pulled him through the crowd on the main floor and to the steel door, pushing it open. The two guys and the chanting acidhead were still there, and as I dragged him down the hall, I stopped, remembering the rules of the place. No fighting. I faced Indy. His eyes were hazy and his shoulders slumped as he stood there, a disgruntled and pissed-off little-boy look on his stoned face. I shoved him against the wall hard, his back thudding against it. His face twisted up in surprise and pain. "Hey, man! What was that for?"

I looked at him for a second, then threw a hard right,

clocking him on the cheekbone. He yelled and went down in a heap, and the two guys at the end of the hall yelled, too. Indy clutched his face. I dropped my board and knelt next to him, getting ready to nail him again as he squirmed, when the huge guy came through the door and ran down the hall.

Big hands reached down and yanked me up; then he threw me against the wall. I kept my feet and faced him, ready. Indy scurried to the side, still holding his face. I nodded to the big guy. "Do it, man. I'll tear you fucking apart."

He sized me up. "I told you no fighting or you're out. Forever."

I readied myself for his fists on my face. It'd be a good fight, but I had no doubt he'd get the best of me. "Maybe it's a good rule." I pointed at Indy. "That's my brother. Beat the shit out of him if you ever see him again."

He glanced at Indy, then back at me, understanding in his hard eyes. He nodded. "Get out or I take you out in pieces." He looked at Indy on the floor. "You too, asshole. Ever come back and I'll break your neck."

I grabbed Indy and pulled him up, and we walked out. Indy didn't say a word until we got to the end of the alley. He cupped a hand over his swollen cheek, spitting blood. "You're a dick."

"So are you."

"There's other places to party."

"So what. I'll come there, too."

"What, are you, like, my guardian fucking angel? I don't need help."

"Who was the girl?"

He shrugged. "I don't know and I don't care."

"You don't even know her name? Are you that high?"

"Whatever, dude. You'd take it if you could get it. And no, I'm not blasted. Just perfect, if you ask me."

"I wouldn't take it from some addict in a room full of scumbags. Ever hear of AIDS?"

"So what."

I grabbed his shoulder and flung him against a brick building. "So what? Why don't you care about anything? You've got a chance, and now you're screwing everything up. Why?"

He looked at me, his face cracking. "Why not? WHY NOT!" He shoved me. "I don't have another chance, Tate, because I've never had one in the first place! Don't you ever think I tried?" He squeezed his head between his hands, rubbing his temples. "Jesus, Tate! It just doesn't click! I CAN'T do it the way they want! Everything gets messed up in my head, and I screw up. School, homework, tests, Dad. All of it."

"Why?"

He laughed, half yelling. "Well, shit, if I knew why, I wouldn't have a problem, would I?"

"You could have a chance, Indy," I said. Then I told him about "Stealing Home," school, and the writing contest.

He shook his head, his mouth an ugly smear. "None of that matters." Tears welled in his eyes, and he looked down. "Just go. Leave me alone."

"No."

He shook his head again. "I know what you did to Will. He's after you now."

"So what?"

"So it's my fault!" he screamed. "I know that! And I know everything else is my fault, but you've got to stay away, Tate. Just stay away."

I shoved him again. "I am so tired of you feeling sorry for yourself! You make me sick, dude, because you have all the choices now! You can come home, go to school, write whatever you want! Dad's not even pissed anymore! You should see them, man! They're just scared. Plain and simple scared for you! So don't be such a prick."

He looked at me. "It's not like that."

"What's not like that?"

His eyes searched mine, fear in them. Pleading. That little brother I'd always known was in those eyes. "I can't get out." He gushed, "I told Will I was splitting. After I got my stuff from the house and you talked to me, I told him I was done." He held back tears. "They'll come after me."

I refused to believe this was happening. "They won't come after you, Indy. Will is just trying to scare you."

He stopped, staring at me with wide eyes. "No, Tate. He's not just trying to scare me. You were right about him. He's crazy."

I looked at him, and there was something in his expression that chilled me to the bone. "What happened to Lucius?"

He looked away.

I sighed. "Jesus, Indy. What do you know?"

He sniffed. "There was nothing I could do. Not like I could stop it."

Slivers of ice stabbed through me. "Oh God." I took a breath. "You're the one in the video?"

He nodded. "Will told me we were going to scare him off. That's it. Next thing I know, he's bashing his brains in. I couldn't do anything."

"You could have gone to the police! That's what!" I groaned, looking up at the night sky. Any idea I had of getting Indy home based on the writing contest was out the window. That was beans compared to this. "Are you that fucking stupid? Jesus, Indy. You're an accessory to murder now."

He shook his head, defeated. "I can't go to the police."

"Why?"

"My fingerprints are on the bat."

"What?"

He nodded. "He wore gloves. Afterward, he pulled a gun out, shoved it in my face, and told me to take the bat. My fingerprints are on it now. Then he told me it was insurance that I was in with them." He looked at me. "I'm in, man, and I can't get out. His uncle has the bat, and if I turn Will in, his uncle will turn over the bat. I'm done."

I clenched my teeth, thinking about the detective. "You've got to come home. We've got to tell Mom and Dad."

"Then what? They kill me or I get charged with murder? Or worse yet, Mom and Dad get hurt? Will is psycho."

"So you're going to get high all the time to deal with it."

He nodded. "If I stay wasted, nothing matters. Better yet, I should just fucking kill myself."

I looked at him, remembering Gregory in "Stealing Home." "Don't say that."

He shook his head. "I should. Everything would be better if I was gone. Mom. Dad. You."

"No."

"Then what? Nothing works, man."

"Then you meet me tomorrow night."

He looked at me. "For what?"

"We'll figure this out." I thought about Ms. Potter. "There's a right way to do this, but we just have to find it."

He swallowed. "Okay. Where?"

I told him.

"Why there?" he said.

"Just meet me. At midnight."

He hesitated. "Fine."

I took his shoulders in my hands. "Make me a promise?"

"What?"

"Don't hurt yourself. You promise?"

His chin quivered just the slightest. "Yeah. I promise."

CHAPTER TWENTY-NINE

With school out for a curriculum day, I stayed inside, thinking about meeting Indy at midnight. Dad was gone before I got up, and Mom was busy in the salon out back all day, so I had the house to myself.

Dad usually got home at five-thirty, and I didn't have it in me to talk to him. So at five, I left, leaving a note for Mom that I wouldn't be home for dinner.

Badger sat behind the counter at the Hole in the Wall, eating Tootsie Rolls. He smiled, his mouth full. "Hey."

"Hey."

He swallowed the gooey brown lump in his mouth, smacking his lips. "How's little skater fellow Mitch?"

I picked up a bong, studying it. "Fine."

"Have you harmed another human being lately?"

"Yeah."

He chuckled. "Here I try to make a joke, and you make it not a joke."

I put the bong back. "You know about the Invitational coming up at the arena?"

He narrowed his eyes. "You mean the Pro Skater Invitational in two weeks to be held at the arena, where local sponsored skaters compete on national television?"

"Yeah, that would be it."

He grabbed a rubber band and pulled his hair back in a ponytail. "I detect an agenda here."

"We need a sponsor."

"Whoa. What happened to the sacred philosophy of not succumbing to the corporate mentality?"

I shrugged. "I think we could win."

"What does that have to do with not succumbing to the corporate mentality?"

I stepped forward, sitting on the stool in front of the counter. "Things change, Badge."

He nodded. "Often they do. Aristotle once noted that principles stand no chance against a good sale at Walmart."

I smiled. "Come on, man. Think about it. We'd have Hole in the Wall shirts and everything. National exposure for you. The entry fee is six hundred bucks, and I have three hundred in my savings account."

"You're serious, aren't you?"

I shrugged again. "Listen, Badge, if I could go pro, what's wrong with it? I'd be doing what I love doing, and making money at it."

He cocked an eye at me. "You slut."

"You know if anybody could beat out your hated

competitor shop, it would be us. Besides, the kid who broke Mitch's board is their top skater."

He smirked. "I'm starting to feel like I'm being manipulated."

I rolled my eyes. "We'd have a shot at it, Badge. You know it. I'd even pay you back the other three hundred when I got it."

"Let me think about it."

I nodded. "Sure."

A moment passed. He stared at me. "What are you doing?"

"Letting you think about it."

"Usually, that means you leave and let me think about it."

I shrugged. "I've got time."

He rolled his eyes. "You want this, huh?"

"Yeah. I really don't have anything to lose at this point, you know? Things are bad everywhere else. I just want to try and do something good."

He narrowed his eyes at me. "This sounds like more than a skate competition."

"Yeah, I guess it is."

"Okay, then. You have a sponsor."

I smiled. "Cool."

• • •

Mom sat in her chair under the lamp, reading one of her novels. She looked up when I shut the door behind me. I set my board by the door. "Hi."

She smiled. "Hi. I was starting to worry."

"I left a note."

"I know, but with everything going on, I'm just nervous." She looked at me, and a heavy pall surrounded her. "Did you see Indy?"

"Yeah. I told him what you and Dad said."

She looked up, the halo of light from the lamp casting her in a soft glow. She looked tired. "What did he say?"

I contemplated telling her what he'd said about Will, but I couldn't. If the police were involved right now, he'd be in even more danger. That didn't make me feel any better about not telling her, though. "He's thinking about it. We're meeting tonight."

She closed her book. "I want to go with you."

I shrugged, sitting on the couch. "He's in with some bad people, Mom. It'd be dangerous right now."

She studied my face. "There's nothing I can do, is there?"

I stared at the carpet for a moment. "Not really. But he told me he wants out. He just has to do it the right way."

"Your father and I put in the missing-person report because we love him. You know that, right?"

"Yeah."

She shook her head, looking down. "I don't care if it's dangerous. Take me to him, Tate."

"I can't, Mom."

Surprisingly, she didn't blink an eye. "Tell him I love him."

"I'm sorry about this. But he does want to make things better."

She smiled, maybe knowing there was nothing more to

say. "There's leftover pot roast in the fridge. Would you take out the garbage after you eat?"

I nodded. "Is Dad asleep?"

She shook her head again. "He's in your room."

I furrowed my brow. "What's he doing in there?"

She gave a wan smile. "Getting to know your brother."

"What?"

She set her hands in her lap and looked at me. "When he got home, he went straight to your room and sat down at Indy's computer, and he's been in there since." She glanced at the clock. "He said he's not coming out until he's read everything his son has written."

"Wow."

She nodded. "He's trying, Tate. I know you're mad at him, but you also know he lives for you two."

I smiled. "I guess I'll be sleeping on the couch. He'll be in there all night."

She smiled, too. "I guess so."

CHAPTER THIRTY

"Do you ever think about him?" I said. With the shadows deep and the moon above casting a monochrome silver over everything, I shivered.

Indy stared at Cutter's grave. "I try not to."

I breathed in the night air, then sat on the grass. "He shouldn't be gone, you know?"

Indy joined me, sitting Indian-style and picking blades of grass. "Why'd you want to meet here?"

I paused, getting my thoughts together. "Cutter didn't just die."

He looked at me. "What?"

"That morning, Cutter got in a huge fight with his mom. Bigger than the usual ones where she yelled and threw him out." I looked at Indy. "She told Cutter he was the reason his dad left them, and that she regretted ever having him in the first place. She said she wished she could take it all back and make him not exist."

Silence. Indy held his breath.

I went on. "He killed himself, Indy. He did it on purpose."

Indy shook his head. "Jesus."

I nodded. "And I was too stupid to see it coming. To help him. I think he told me about the fight because he knew what he was going to do. To sort of give a reason."

His voice came like a ghost in the deserted cemetery. "Why are you telling me this?"

"Because I'm not going to lose you, too. We have more than Cutter ever did, Indy. Dad might be a jerk, but he loves us. Loves you," I said. I told him that Dad had been in our room reading all his stuff. "He just does things differently." I looked at him. "You know he loves you, right?"

Indy lowered his head. "How come I always screw up, Tate?"

"It's not about screwing up. It's about screwing up and trying to figure out how to fix it." I paused, and the night seemed to pause with me. "Look at his headstone, Indy."

Indy raised his head, looking at Cutter's name etched in the marble. A tear slid down his cheek. "I miss him."

"Me too. But I'm not going to visit my brother here. Not like this. Not because he gave up."

A sob racked his chest, and he lowered his head, rocking back and forth, crying. "It would be so much easier if I was gone. Haven't you ever just felt like . . . being gone?"

"Yeah. And that's why we're here. Cutter wouldn't want this, Indy. He'd tell you you're crazy for thinking like that, and he'd help."

"I can't get out," he said, sniffing. "The only thing I can do is stay so high that it makes it hurt less, so I do." He laughed. "I'm even too chickenshit to kill myself."

"You can get out. And you will. And you're not going to kill yourself, either."

"How can I get out?"

I looked at him, then at Cutter's headstone. Then I told him.

CHAPTER THIRTY-ONE

After school the next day, I skated Under the Bridge alone, my mind full of a weird nothingness . . . just an almost-overwhelming anxiety that wouldn't let me focus on anything. Two words kept running through my head, though. *The bat.*

The Monster was empty, so I headed over and stood on the edge, looking down. Skating a vert is like dancing. It flows. You feel like you're making something when you carve back and forth, and the more you get into the movements, the more life seems to disappear around you.

You can start out on edge or depressed or pissed off about something, but after a while it takes you and empties your mind of everything but the wheels vibrating below you and the lines you cut across the space, and that's why I love it. It's peace.

I'd pulled a seven-twenty once before, but I'd never even tried a nine hundred. Tony Hawk invented the nine hundred when I was a little kid, and I remembered seeing him do it on TV once. Not many guys who weren't pro could do it—but, I thought as I skated, nobody was born a pro.

I rolled back and forth on the vert, threw down a backside ollie-to-tail and a couple of easy rock-and-rolls, then ran into a frontside varial revert and hit a varial five-forty smooth as ice on the flip side, my mind getting into my line and my ride getting into my bones.

I knew I couldn't do a nine hundred, but I'd been working on a gymnast handplant. Although it was tricky to nail down, I was able to do it and come off solid. After that, I crossed over a few times, built up some speed, and put a good four feet of air under my wheels in an airwalk that I'd learned last year. I hit the edge on the other side, flipped my board up, and noticed Detective Connelly sitting on a bench, watching me.

I stood there catching my breath for a minute or two, watching the park clear as kids headed home for dinner or homework or nagging parents. I walked over, sitting next to him. "Like skate parks, huh?"

Detective Connelly smiled. "My son skates. He's twelve."

"Cool."

"You're good."

"Thanks. I'm planning on trying to go pro."

He cleared his throat. "So, you called me. What's on your mind?"

CHAPTER THIRTY-TWO

Darkness surrounded Indy and me as we crouched behind a pile of garbage in the vacant lot behind the old apartment building, and the only thing we'd seen this late was a bum passing through the alley separating us from the building and a cat slinking around hunting rats.

I looked at Indy in the darkness. "You're absolutely sure Will's uncle lives here?"

"Yeah. His uncle Vernon told me the address himself."

"Zero-two-niner, this is the Sidonator. Do you copy, Flying Turdbuckets? Do you copy?"

I held the two-way radio, wondering what in the heck Sid was talking about. "What?"

Positioned in front of the building, dressed as a homeless guy and sitting next to a shopping cart he'd lifted from a Safeway down the road, he whispered into the radio, "Code. That's the way they talk during covert operations, man. Get with it."

I rolled my eyes, not in the mood for Sid's sarcasm. My stomach roiled as I thought about what we had to do. "Everything is fine. Is his car still out there?"

"That's affirmative, Turd. Surveillance has shown Bad Evil Dude's vehicle is still parked at the curb."

"Okay," I said.

His voice came scratchy through the radio. "Give me the word and we're on. Piper is waiting."

I looked at Indy. "You ready?"

He took a breath, then nodded.

I spoke into the radio. "Okay. We'll need a few minutes."

His voice whispered through the receiver. "Pipopotamus is on standby."

"Okay. And remember, you've got to tell us if he starts to go back inside."

Sid took a moment. "Dude, I got a bad feeling about this."

"It'll work," I said. "Just don't lose your cool."

I clipped the radio on my belt and stood, stretching my legs. "Let's go."

Indy stood, following me along the alley to a huge storage container against the apartment building. I hopped on a stack of crates next to a Dumpster, then balanced on the edge of the green bin, jumping up to grab the edge of the container and pulling myself up. Once on top of the container, I padded down to the fire escape ladder, which hung four feet from where I stood. Indy followed me, shaking his head. I saw that we'd have to jump across the span to grab the ladder.

Adrenaline pumped through me as I took a few steps back

and ran, jumping the distance and slamming into the metal ladder. Just before I fell, I looped my arm through a rung and hung, windmilling my feet in the empty space below and throwing my other arm up and through another rung. Scrunching up my legs, I got a foot through the bottom rung and pulled myself up. I looked back at Indy. "You come when I get to the first landing," I whispered.

Sweat beaded on my forehead, and a drip, slow and itchy, ran down into my eye, burning like acid. I wiped it on my shoulder and climbed the wobbly metal rungs, trying to be as quiet as possible. When I reached the first floor, I sat on the metal grated landing and caught my breath. This was crazy. Insane.

I looked at Indy, and he hesitated. We were too far away to risk talking, so I motioned for him. No time to be a pussy, Indy. Come on. You can do it. A moment later, Indy was flying through the air, flailing as he reached for the ladder. With a rattle, he banged his arm through the rung, grunting with the impact.

I looked up. Two more floors before we could reach the ledge that would take us to his window. I sighed, thinking we should just go to the door, bust it in, take the bat, and run, but I couldn't risk the plan.

With Indy following, I climbed to the next level, stopping when a light in a window next to the ladder went on. I smashed myself against the wall, waiting several minutes before the light went off, then continued up, my hands coated with red rust from the weathered metal and my breath coming heavy.

Ten minutes later, we crouched on the landing of the third floor, looking over the side rail at the ledge running the length of the building. Not more than a foot wide. I stared at it, almost chickening out, then climbed the rail and stepped onto it.

My mind raced. On any day of the week, I could walk a straight line on a twelve-inch-wide board with my eyes closed, but forty feet up and with fear and adrenaline streaking through me like a million bolts of lightning, I shook. My legs felt like wet spaghetti noodles, and my pulse must have been at over two hundred. I felt like I was going to have a heart attack.

Beside me on the ledge, Indy whispered in my ear, "This is so not right, man. Crazy."

"We can do this. We have to," I said, inching my way to the corner of the building, staying flat against the brick, and peeking around to the alley. Nobody was down there, and I could see the glow from a streetlight at the entrance. Down one long wall, less than fifteen yards away, was the window. It seemed like a million miles.

I rounded the corner, trying not to look down, and slid my way along, going as fast as I could. Ten minutes later, we were there. With the shades closed, I risked peeking down at the window latch. Relief spread through me. It was unlocked. No cars rolled down the street, and only a few people wandered down the sidewalks, so I unclipped the radio. "We're here, Sid. Tell Piper to do his thing," I whispered.

Closing my eyes, I counted. Piper should be skating down the street right now, hammer in hand. Ten. Eleven. Twelve.

CRASH. The sound of Piper smashing the windshield of Will's uncle's car reached us, and a second later, the car alarm screeched.

A light flipped on in the apartment, and we heard rustling inside, then cussing. Half a minute later, we heard a door slam shut. I pushed the button on the radio. "He should be out in a minute."

"Roger dodger. Piper's long gone."

We waited. I looked at Indy. "We have to find it quick. Real quick."

He nodded, his face pale in the shadows.

Sid's voice crackled through the radio. "He's out. Go."

I held my breath, hooked my fingers on the frame of the window, and lifted gently. It slid up. In another few seconds I had it wide open, so I crouched, moving the curtain to the side and peeking into the living room. Empty. I twisted on the ledge, sliding a leg inside, and a moment later I was standing on the carpet. Indy followed. I shut the curtain. "You take the kitchen. Look everywhere, but try not to make it look like we were here."

The first thing I noticed was that the nondescript, plain apartment was clean. Immaculate. No signs of living in it besides a pillow on a couch. No dirty dishes, cigarette butts littering ashtrays, empty burger wrappers, nothing. I unclipped the radio from my belt and whispered into it, "We're in."

Tension laced Sid's voice, which was strange. "Hurry. You should see him. He's sooo pissed. Cussing and yelling and shit."

I swept through the living room, knowing the last thing a drug dealer would do would be to call the cops. I heard the alarm shut off, then glanced at Indy ripping through the cupboards, my pulse rising once again. We had minutes. I ran to the bedroom.

A single T-shirt on the crumpled bed and scattered change on the nightstand were the only signs of life. After a minute of going through the clothes in the drawers, I checked the closet and under the bed. No bat. Nothing.

Back in the living room, I checked under the couches, threw the pillow on the floor, and found nothing but dust and a few pennies. My heart sank. Either it wasn't here or it was in the kitchen, so I padded over, joining Indy. He frantically searched. We'd been in the apartment for less than five minutes.

He opened the oven, checked it, then shut the door. "Fuck. It's not here."

I looked around. "You checked everything? Under the sink?"

He nodded, and Sid's voice crackled through the radio. "He just went back inside. Get out."

I pressed the button. "We didn't find it."

"Dude, get out. Now. You've got, like, three minutes."

My heart caught in my throat, and as I turned back toward the living room to bolt for the window, my eye caught the only place I hadn't checked. The refrigerator. I grabbed the sides. "Help. Hurry."

Indy grabbed the sides, too, and we worked the box away

from the wall. After a minute, I was able to reach behind it, and as I did, my fingers hit something. Angling my arm further back, I wrapped my fingers around it. "I got it," I said, pulling the plastic-wrapped bat out. I handed it to him. "Let's go."

Indy ran for the window as I shoved the refrigerator back. Just then, the doorknob squeaked as it turned. I was in direct sight of the door. I motioned at Indy, who had one leg out the window. "Go, man. Get out!" I whispered frantically.

He stared at the door as it swung open, then lifted his leg back inside, staring at me. "I'm not leaving."

There was only one solution. It was football time. I looked at Indy. "Follow me." As the door opened, I ran, sprinting down the short hall toward it. Just as Will's uncle stepped inside, I hit him high and hard like a linebacker going in for the kill: elbows up, forearms crossed. I nailed him solid in the chest and he flew back, his feet in the air as he slammed against the wall of the hall outside.

I didn't stop, and we ran. Just as we hit the stairwell at the end of the hall, I glanced back. Vernon was on his feet, pulling a pistol from his waistband. He staggered after us. I grabbed Indy. "Come on."

We took the stairs three at a time, grabbing the railing for balance as we ran and jumped and scrabbled downward. I could hear Vernon following, and was surprised he'd even gotten up after a hit like that. As we reached the first floor, Indy let out a yelp and I stopped, turning around as he tumbled ass-over-head to my feet. He groaned. I grabbed him, yanking him to his feet. He still held the bat. "You okay?"

He grimaced, gasping in pain, then looked down. "Fuck."

I looked down. His foot was angled sideways. Completely destroyed. "It's broken."

"Fuck. We're dead," he said, clenching his teeth.

With the sound of Vernon running down the staircase behind us, I took a breath, then picked Indy up. "Nothing to do but try. Put your arm around my neck, and don't let go of the bat," I said, then ran through the lobby of the building, carrying him.

We hit the doors and I took a sharp right, hoping to get around the corner to the alley before Vernon saw which way we went. It was no use, though. Just as we rounded the corner, I heard the doors slam open, then running feet coming our way. I looked around in the dark, and there was nothing but the alley. Nowhere to hide. We were screwed.

"Why are you carrying your brother?"

Startled, I turned to the other side of the alley. "What the fu—?"

Dad stood there, his work clothes still on. "Your mother told me you were meeting with Indy. I followed you, then lost you, then saw Piper skating. . . ." Then he whipped his head around as Vernon, pistol in hand, charged around the corner. Dad stepped between us and him, facing the man.

Vernon came to a halt, raising the pistol.

My dad lifted his hands to him. "Whoa. Slow down there, buddy. Put the weapon down."

Confusion spread over Vernon's face, but he didn't waver. "Who're you?"

"I'm these boys' father. Put the weapon down."

Vernon shook his head. "Give me the bat and everything will be fine."

Dad glanced back at us, confusion on his face. He looked at the packaged bat. "Indy, throw him the bat."

My heart raced, and my mind reeled. "Will used it to kill Lucius, then made Indy hold it. His prints are on it for insurance. They'll think Indy did it. He was the kid in the video," I blurted out.

It took a second for my words to register in his head, but the picture was there. He took a great breath, his chest and shoulders expanding. He stared at Vernon. "Let's talk about this. Find a solution."

Vernon smiled. "Your kid has been nothing but a pain in my ass. Give me the bat."

Silence followed in the darkness. Then Dad spoke. "You're not hurting my boys."

Vernon cocked the pistol. Dad rushed him. I dropped Indy.

The shot rang out as Dad closed in, but he didn't stop. A look of surprise crossed Vernon's face when Dad didn't go down, and the next thing he knew, Dad plowed into him.

They both went down in a heap, Dad's huge fists digging into Vernon's rib cage as he struggled to get away. As I ran toward them, another shot rang out, this one muffled. Blood pooled beneath them. Then I saw my dad's hand wrap around Vernon's, pinning the pistol against the ground. I saw my dad's elbow jacking into Vernon's face furiously. The drug dealer's body went limp. Then I was there.

I scrambled around them, grabbing the pistol and yanking it from Vernon's hand, then throwing it across the alley. Dad lay on top of the man, his chest heaving. I touched his shoulder, fear ripping through me. "Dad."

He put his palm on the ground for support, then rolled from the unconscious Vernon, whose face was a mess from the elbow hits. Both men were covered in blood. Panic swept through me as I knelt. Indy, his ankle mangled, hopped to us, then fell to his knees beside me. Dad stared at the darkened sky, breathing heavily. We heard sirens in the distance. Dad grunted. "Bastard got me good."

Indy leaned over him. "Jesus, Tate. He's shot."

Dad looked at Indy, his eyes glassy. "You clean that bat handle off and give it to the police when they get here. You hear me? Do it right, Indy. Do the right thing. You're my son."

Tears slid down Indy's face. "Dad, no. You can't go. I fucked up so bad. You can't."

Dad closed his eyes. "Go home tonight, son. Be with your mother."

CHAPTER THIRTY-THREE

"He's in critical but stable condition. The surgery is done, and your mother is with him." Detective Connelly sat behind the table. Indy and I sat facing him. We were waiting for an attorney to show up. He went on, looking at me, "When you told me that you would 'turn in' the murder weapon, you didn't tell me how you'd do it."

I shrugged. "I want to see my dad."

"You will. We just need a statement, and to make it legal, you need an attorney present because you're minors. Your mother gave consent at the hospital."

Indy shook his head. "I told you. Will murdered Lucius with the bat. I saw it. I'll testify."

The detective nodded. "I appreciate that, but we have to make it legal. I know you boys want to see your father, but until we get your statement, I have to detain you. Policy."

I cleared my throat. "What about Will's uncle?"

"He's being charged with attempted first-degree murder

for shooting your father. With his record, and the charges that will follow, he won't see daylight again."

"And Will?"

"Based on testimony from Indy, he'll be charged with murder in the first degree." He looked at us. "That is, when we find him."

I furrowed my brow. "You can't find him?"

"He disappeared. Don't worry, though, we'll get him."

I shook my head. "He'll be after Indy."

"He probably fled the area," he said. Then the door opened.

A fat, balding man, disheveled and angry-looking, walked in. "It's three-thirty in the morning. What am I doing here?"

Detective Connelly looked at us. "Indy, start talking."

CHAPTER THIRTY-FOUR

Indy wouldn't leave the hospital, and every time I looked at him, I could see what he was feeling. Guilt, pain, relief, sadness. He and Dad talked privately for long hours, and I could tell that something had changed in my brother. Maybe he had learned that life could be for keeps and that sometimes it could turn out for the worst.

As usual, Mom was the rock of the family. My dad had always gotten the credit for being the tough guy, and she had always stood in the shadows, but I realized that she was something altogether different. Something that I'd always taken advantage of without knowing it. She held everything together. When there was no reasoning, she was the reasonable one. When tempers flared, she was the voice that kept us together. She was the one who made our family function, and I looked at her in a new way.

Two days after the incident, school let out and I skated three blocks to the hospital. Indy was just leaving Dad's room, awkwardly working his crutches. He smiled. "He's coming home tomorrow."

I slapped him five. "Cool." I looked at him. "You coming back to school?"

He leaned against the wall. "Eventually. Mom is talking to them, and it looks like I'll be able to be in Mr. Halvorson's English class. But the police told her that I should stay home until they find Will."

"They'll find him," I said.

He shook his head. "I know Will, Tate. He didn't leave town."

I clenched my teeth. "Then we'll deal with it as it comes, but they'll find him. They will."

He looked down, shook his head, then smiled. "Whatever, dude, but I heard something else."

"What?"

He looked at me. "The skate Invitational. Piper told me you guys are in it. Badger's sponsoring?"

I nodded. "Yeah."

"Why didn't you tell me?"

I laughed, looking away. "Other things were going on."

He shook his head. "You've got to stop it."

"Stop what?"

"You always take care of other people, Tate. Mostly me." He studied my face. "It's time for you to do this for you. You could go pro."

"You hate corporate," I said.

He chuckled. "I don't hate it as much as I'd like to see my brother kick ass."

I smiled.

He came forward then and gave me an awkward hug.

"What was that for?"

He stuffed his hands in his pockets. "I don't know, man. Maybe because you saved my life. Maybe because I'm a selfish asshole and I don't want to be one anymore."

I laughed. "You *can* be quite the asshole."

He hit my shoulder. "Back at ya. I'm going to Burger King. Dad's got a hankering for a burger."

I nodded. "I'm out in a bit. Just stopping by to say hello to him. We're meeting at the Monster tonight. Practice again."

"Cool. See ya, huh?"

I opened the door. "Yeah. See ya. And be careful."

CHAPTER THIRTY-FIVE

The night air whipped through my hair, and the echo of my wheels on the Monster filled my ears, as I finally laid down a seven-twenty without a hitch. Piper sat on the edge watching, and he flipped me the thumbs-up as I grinned. Sid lit a cigarette as I hit the edge for a breather. We'd been practicing hard-core every night for three to six hours. It was also the only way I could get the threat of Will out of my head. "Tomorrow night's the night, guys."

Sid lay back, staring at the underside of the bridge and exhaling. "Too bad Indy's a cripple."

I shrugged. "I don't think he'd do it even without a broken ankle."

"When's he coming back to school?"

"Depends on Will. Mom had to meet with the school to get the truancy stuff all straightened out."

"Will would be an idiot to stay in town, man. He's probably in Texas by now," Piper said.

Sid, still staring at the bridge above him, picked his nose and flicked the booger. "I heard he's around."

My stomach squirmed. "From who?"

"Michael."

"Shit."

Sid took a swig of Mountain Dew. "Shit's right. You know why he's still here, huh?"

"Indy."

Sid nodded. "Serious stuff, man. He *knows* Indy is the only witness."

"Yeah."

Piper chomped on a stick of beef jerky. His midnight snack. "You guys should lay low until the cops get him. Have they said anything?"

I shook my head. "Nope. They patrol by the house every hour, and my mom has talked to them about it, but there's not much to do."

Piper shook his head. "Witness protection. I wonder if you can pick your own name."

I laughed. "Yeah, right. This is a small-time thing, not some big federal gig. And they said Indy wouldn't be the deciding factor if they could get Will's DNA or fingerprints from the bat."

Piper chewed his jerky. "How'd that work out, anyway? With Indy's prints?"

"He took the bat out of the plastic before the cops came and was holding it when they got there," I said. In our statement, we hadn't mentioned that Will had made Indy touch the weapon, and now, with the cops knowing that Indy had touched it after the fact, he wouldn't be implicated.

Sid laughed. "Wow. You so smart, Kemo Sabe."

I nodded. "I've got an idea."

Piper grimaced, glancing at Sid. "Crap. You know what this means, Sid? Every idea he gets has to do with possible death."

I shook my head. "Not yours. Just mine." I looked at Sid. "I want you to tell Michael that Indy wants to score some dope tomorrow night at one-thirty. At the Monster."

Piper shook his head, chewing with his mouth open. "You're nuts."

I shrugged. "I'm serious."

Sid hesitated. "Tate . . ."

"Just do it, huh? You know he'll tell Will, and I'll take care of the rest. Just don't say anything to Indy."

• • •

When I came home forty-five minutes later, Indy sat at his desk, his fingers flying over the keyboard. I smiled. "Not at the hospital, huh?"

He stopped typing. "Dad kicked me out. Told me to stop feeling guilty and move on." He looked at me. "How was practice?"

I dropped my board and lay down on my bed, glancing at his desk. A fat tube of pepper spray sat on it. "Good. Piper's really ripping it up." I motioned to the spray. "Where'd you get that?"

"Mom got us all one," he said, pointing to my nightstand, where another spray was. "Dad had me unlock his shotgun and put it in their room, too, but Mom unloaded it. She said it's dangerous in the house without somebody who knows how to use it right, and Dad is the only one who took a defense class on it."

"Looks like we're Fort Brooks, then."

He shrugged. "I'm under unofficial house arrest until they find him."

"That's a good idea. Sid heard he's around."

Indy picked up the tube of spray. "I almost wish he'd come. Just to get it over with. It's freaking me out."

"He might be evil, but he's not stupid. The cops are all over this neighborhood." Changing the subject, I said, "How's Dad?"

"Fine. Pissed off that he can't go to work."

"Figures."

Indy nodded. "He told me that he's going to the Invitational no matter what any doctor says."

I smiled. "Cool."

"You can do it, Tate."

I hopped on my bed. "We'll see."

"You win the Invitational, I'll get straight A's for the rest of the year if I can. Deal?"

I smiled again. "Deal." I took a breath, tempted to tell him what I was going to do Under the Bridge, but there was no need. It would just put him at risk. "They'll get him, Indy. Then you'll be in school getting those A's."

CHAPTER THIRTY-SIX

Kimberly Lawson and I stood across the street from the arena. Badger—along with giving the three of us the T-shirts he had made—had set us up with extra boards, shrugging and telling us that if we were going to represent the Hole in the Wall, we'd better do it with some sort of style. I looked up at the huge building. "Well, here we are."

She smiled, then took my hand in hers, squeezing. "My parents are coming."

I looked at her.

She nodded. "I told them I was dating a soon-to-be-pro skater."

I frowned. "I'm sure they were thrilled."

"My mom had a fit because she's sure you're a criminal, but my dad . . ." She paused, smiling.

"What?"

"He told me that the only thing that mattered was that I was happy. He wants to meet you."

"Wow."

"I know. I think he realized after I quit the violin that I lived my life around them. Either that or he's scared to death I'm serious about you."

I led her across the street. "I say let him be scared."

She laughed. "I say there's nothing to be scared of. He'll see that today." Then she turned to me. "Look for me, huh? I'll be waving a big banner with *Tate Brooks Rocks* on it."

I kissed her then, and it wasn't a goodbye kiss. It was a great kiss. A fantastic one. One that I never wanted to end. "We'll see you."

She smiled. "Excited?"

I looked at the building. "Crapping my pants, actually."

She laughed again. "You can do it, street boy. I know you can." Then she was gone, walking across the street and around the corner.

CHAPTER THIRTY-SEVEN

"Tate Brooks. Hole in the Wall." I showed my registration ticket to the lady at the rear entrance, then looked around for the crew. The loading area of the arena was full of semitrucks, drivers, security, roadies, and a small group of pro skaters who, true to their nature, took turns dropping in off a loading dock, their boards clattering as they hit the pavement.

The lady checked my name off a list, handed me a plastic ALL-ACCESS SKATER pass with my name on it, and opened the door. She smiled. "Good luck."

"Thank you." I looped the pass over my neck and walked down a hall to the staging area. People milled around, and a kid—probably thirteen and wearing a RESTRICTED ACCESS sticker—ran under a rope barrier and up to me, a board in one hand and a black marker in the other.

He held out the pen, excitement in his eyes. "Sign it for me, please?"

I looked at his board. "I'm not—"

"Please? I can't go over there." He pointed toward some offices, where four or five pro skaters sat on black metal road bins.

I looked at him, thinking of Mitch the grom. "Here. I'll do you one better. Come on." Then I walked with him over to the skaters. They saw the board in my hands and the skater card around my neck and stopped talking. I knew each and every one of them from all the mags I had stashed in my room. The pros. "Hey."

One nodded to me. "Local?"

"Yeah."

A couple of the guys snickered, but he didn't. "Cool. Good luck, man." He pointed to a room. "That's the locals' joint. You'll be staged from there."

"Thanks." I hesitated. "Hey, listen, would you mind signing his board? And mine, actually?"

The guy looked at the boy, then nodded. "Sure, man. Here, give them over."

So we did, and they passed the two boards around, each signing the bottoms of the decks. The kid was almost hyperventilating by the time I walked him back to the rope. He turned, said thanks, then handed me his board. "You didn't sign."

I looked at him, then at the board. "I'm not a pro."

He smiled. "I know. You're from here, though. Just sign it, huh?"

I did, scrawling my name on the deck. "There you go."

He beamed. "Cool. Thanks." Then he scrambled under the rope.

I turned toward the offices.

"Hey." The boy's voice came again. I turned back, and he flashed me another smile. "Kick their asses, okay?"

I smiled. "I'll try," I said. And I would try.

CHAPTER THIRTY-EIGHT

"Holy shit," Sid whispered as we stood on the second level looking down on the vert planted on the arena floor. The butterflies in the pit of my stomach turned into burrowing rats. *Holy shit* was right. From above, the sweeping wooden surface of the U-shaped structure looked huge.

I took a breath, staring at the skaters warming up below, dropping in, taking turns as the seats of the arena filled. "We should warm up, guys. It starts in an hour."

Piper cleared his throat. "I shouldn't be scared, right? We can handle this, right? Why am I peeing my pants? Jesus, look at that." He put his hands on the rail, bowing his head between them. "I'm going to puke, guys."

I laughed. "We can handle—" Before I could finish, he did. All over the floor. Half-digested day-old deli sandwich minus lettuce splattered on his shoes. I stepped back as scores of people walking by gaped and gawked, disgust on their faces.

Piper wiped his mouth, sighing. "Better now."

Sid, unperturbed, called for a cleanup on aisle five. I shook my head. "Dude . . ."

Piper smiled. "Got any gum?"

"Let's go. Once the competition starts, we've each got one run. A minute and a half to pull every trick we know without screwing up and making fools of ourselves in front of the entire country." We walked back to the hall circling the arena, past security at the entrance, and made our way to the floor. We stopped, looking up at the seats as they filled. I felt small. Minuscule. One run. Ninety seconds. One shot at making it.

Piper pointed up. "Hey, there's my barf."

I looked up, and a maintenance guy was dragging a mop back and forth. Off to the right, I noticed an ESPN camera crew setting up gear. The burrowing rats in my stomach became clawing tigers. "Come on. Take as many practice runs as you can, guys."

We passed through the freestyle-trick area and climbed the stairs to the platform on top of the vert. I stood at the coping on the edge and looked down. Bigger than the Monster. Steeper. Pure fear hit me, my nerves frayed and sweat building on my brow.

The pros were gone now, their practice runs taken care of, and that left the vert for the amateurs. I looked across the bowl to the other side, and there, on the opposing platform, were Corey and his crew. He smiled, then laughed as he spread his arms wide, gesturing for me to go first.

Piper grumbled, "What a prick."

I shook my head. "Don't pay attention to him, Pipe. Just skate."

Piper dropped his board to the deck. "You go first, chief. This was your grand idea."

I didn't bother telling him he was the one who brought it up first. I set my board down, adjusted my knee and elbow pads, balanced my tail on the coping, and, with a small prayer to the anti-humiliation gods, dropped in. And proceeded to slide out and burn my ass on the wood all the way down.

Corey and his crew, all but Stick, laughed. Once I stopped sliding, I grabbed my board and walked off, back up the stairs. My cheeks burned, and sweat poured from under my helmet as I reached the crew. Sid smirked. "Nice start, Tate, but we're not sledding."

I sighed, my eyes going to the seats. Three-quarters of them were filled. Thousands of people would be watching me. I closed my eyes. Come on, Tate. Ignore it. Just skate. Let it happen. I opened my eyes as Corey dropped in from the other side, carving a straight line, building incredible speed, coming up our side, doing a simple turn, and shooting back down. I swallowed. "The wood is slicker than the concrete, guys. Be careful."

After Corey finished his run, Piper dropped in, wobbling a bit but keeping his wheels on the downside. He carved back and forth two times, then hit his first trick, nailing it with that shit-eating grin on his face that said he was in his groove. Sid actually laughed. "I thought we were doomed there for a minute with your grand entrance. At least one of us can stay upright."

"Thanks, Sid."

"At least Puke Boy kept his ass off the deck."

When it was my turn again, I tailed off the coping and dropped in, this time ignoring everything except the feel of my board on the deck and the flow of my wheels rolling. Fast. Faster than I'd ever experienced on a vert. I hit a simple turn on the first run and then, back on our side, held my breath and pulled off an airwalk, landing it without a bump. There. You can do it, man. It's just bigger. Faster. All the same but bigger.

I finished my last run with a trick that brought scattered applause from the preshow crowd, and felt a flush of excitement course through me. Sid and Pipe slapped me five, and Stick yelled out from across the vert, "Nice, Tate. Nice."

I waved to him, and we spent the next thirty-five minutes taking turns getting used to the deck. Then a lady wearing a STAFF shirt waved us down. Warm-ups were over. I glanced at the digital clock under the big-screen monitor. Fifteen minutes until it started. The shakes came back. Fifteen minutes.

CHAPTER THIRTY-NINE

Our staging room was too small for us and Corey's crew. The universe was too small for Corey, and within ten minutes, I knew there'd be a fist-fight. Corey was at his finest, slinging barbs across the room, and Piper, so high on adrenaline his eyes were twittering, slung shit back at him with abandon. I stood. "I'm checking the show out. See ya."

Sid was sprawled on the floor staring at the ceiling and Piper hashed back and forth with Corey as I left. I walked to the floor entrance, the music blaring and the crowd roaring as the pros came out for their introductions, pulling a couple of tricks each as the announcer hyped the crowd up.

I watched, and a moment later, Stick came up beside me and watched, too. He smiled. "Sort of a trip, huh?"

I nodded.

"Indy's not competing."

"No."

He nodded. "He's got style."

"He'd eat it up here."

Stick stuffed his hands in his pockets. "I've been watching you guys."

"Oh yeah?"

He nodded again. "Yeah, and our crew is better than yours, even if Corey is full of crap."

I smiled. "Looking for a fight?"

"No, I'm not, but we're better." He looked at me. "Without Indy backing you, we'll win."

I laughed. "Indy backing me? You've got that wrong. I'd be backing him."

He shook his head. "You're a better skater than any of us. Better than Indy. You just don't know it."

I stared out across the packed arena. "Yeah, right."

His eyes met mine. "Corey's skating after you. He's the last skater." He paused. "You've got one run, Tate, and you can beat him. You can take the Best Amateur Individual, and sponsors will be calling your number."

"Why are you telling me this?"

He shrugged. "My own reasons, but you won't see me skating with Corey or the Wheelhouse after this. I'm sick of his shit."

"Looking for a new crew?"

"Maybe, but Corey is your competition tonight, because he's good. Good enough to go pro. And he's going to be pulling some monster shit." He paused, raising his voice as the first pro skater took the vert to thunderous applause. He went on, "If you go light, he'll beat you out. That's all I wanted to say." Then he slapped me on the shoulder and walked away.

CHAPTER FORTY

"LADIES AND GENTLEMEN," the announcer blared, "WE HAVE THREE LOCAL SPONSORED TEAMS OF SKATERS HERE WITH US TONIGHT, AND THEY'RE HERE TO SHOW YOU WHAT THEY HAVE!!!! PLEASE WELCOME TEAM WHEELHOUSE, TEAM HOLE IN THE WALL, AND TEAM POST FALLS, FROM NEIGHBORING POST FALLS, IDAHO!!! LET THEM HEAR YOU, SPOKAAAANE!!!"

Piper yelled as he followed me up to the platform and the crowd went crazy, "I'm gonna puke again, man."

I laughed, yelling back, "Just don't get any on me." It was so incredibly loud I could barely hear myself. Volbeat pounded the song "Thanks" over the speakers at our introduction, and as I reached the platform with the Post Falls team, I scanned the crowd, finding Indy, my parents, and Bill Badger in the section they'd told me to look in. Mitch the grom sat next to Badger. Everybody except my dad was standing, screaming their lungs out and waving to get my attention. I smiled, waving back, and Mom put her hands over her mouth, which meant she was crying.

My eyes went over the rest of the crowd until I found Kimberly, holding up her TATE BROOKS ROCKS sign. Her parents were beside her, with her father standing and clapping and her mother sitting sullenly. I waved, smiling and laughing through my nervousness.

Then the announcer spoke again. "LADIES AND GENTLEMEN, EACH SKATER WILL HAVE ONE RUN TO PROVE JUST HOW GOOD SPOKANE SKATERS ARE!!! BUT WE HAVE A LITTLE SURPRISE FOR YOU HERE TONIGHT!!! SHOULD I TELL YOU WHAT IT IS?" The crowd roared and he went on. "FLYING GECKO SKATEBOARDS OUT OF MARINA DEL REY, CALIFORNIA, ONE OF THE PRIMO BOARD COMPANIES IN THE WORLD, IS OFFERING A FULL SPONSORSHIP TO THE INDIVIDUAL AMATEUR SKATE WINNER THIS EVENING!!!!"

My jaw dropped, and the claws in my stomach ripped me to shreds. No way. Pro. I could go pro tonight. No phone calls, no working my way up the circuit. Tonight. Dizziness swept over me as I realized what the stakes were, and I steadied myself. Pipe and Sid grinned ear to ear, waving to the crowd as the announcer introduced the first skater, Stick from the Wheelhouse.

With "Breadfan" from Metallica machine-gunning over the sound system, Stick dropped in and pulled his first trick, a rock-and-roll, then carved to the other side, pulled a three-sixty frontside to thunderous approval from the crowd, barely hung on to a Stalefish, pulled a couple of minor filler tricks, gained speed two times through, and ended with a Switch Indy Air, pivoting, spinning, and landing it with ease. He was on his game.

Piper nodded to the beat as we watched, yelling in my ear, "*Stakes are high and so am I, got me a rock-and-roll band, it's a free-for-all.* I'm next, mofo. Wish me luck."

I laughed at his Ted Nugent lyrics, and as that song by the Nuge began—the song he'd picked for his run—he tailed in and went for it, wiping Stick all over the floor with a huge airwalk followed by a Stalefish seven-twenty finale. I hooted and hollered, caught up in the excitement as he shredded. The announcer blared props for Hole in the Wall, and I glanced up at Mom and Dad, who sat next to Badger. Badge smiled, holding up his arms and taking all the credit as he nodded his big fat head. I laughed, realizing I was having a blast. This was for me, I knew. I could get used to this.

On down the line they went, calling each name. Sid picked it up a notch even for him, although Piper's run had been better. But at the last turn, Sid took a digger, sliding on his knees as the crowd quieted. Piper leaned toward me. "The Wheelhouse just won, dude. Post Falls boys aren't that good, but that just screwed us."

I took a deep breath, ignoring him. We could win. Just me and Corey were left, and if Corey fell, we might take it. I thought about what Stick told me. Monster shit. I had to do it. This wasn't just about me and my future and what I wanted

244

so badly; it was about us. All of us. The crew. Indy. Cutter. Then the announcer said my name, the crowd cheered, and my favorite song by Volbeat, "Sad Man's Tongue," hammered the speakers and pumped me full of adrenalized electricity. This was it. I tailed on the coping and looked down.

I knew what I had to do. No filler tricks, keep my speed, and kill it. All monsters. One run, one chance. I took a deep breath, steadied myself, then dropped in when the first heavy guitar riff pounded the speakers.

I flew, and I forgot everything but the music smashing through me and my wheels flying. The crowd, the roar, my parents, Kimberly, Will—everything disappeared in a moment, and I knew I was meant for this. Meant to skate. Meant to carve and grind and fly and meant to be *good* at something. Strength burned through me as I hit the coping, driving straight into a huge airwalk right in front of Corey's face.

I nailed it solid, crouching for speed, then hit the other side, spinning straight into the biggest three-sixty frontside rock-and-roll I'd ever done. In the distance I heard the crowd roar, and the moment my wheels hit the landing, I crouched again, straight as an arrow as I sped across and up the vert, launching into a mammoth varial five-forty.

Shooting across the deck after the varial five-forty, I barely pulled out a gymnast handplant, to the astonishment of the announcer. The only thing I heard over the muffled noise was "THIS YOUNG MAN WANTS IT, LADIES AND GENTLEMEN!!!!"

I was completely in the zone. Outside of myself. Not

seeing, not hearing, just feeling it. Feeling the roll of the board and the flow of the dance and the feeling in my chest that no person could explain and that I loved so much. I carved the vert twice, gaining speed and pulling a Stalefish seven-twenty. The crowd went crazy when I landed it, and I glanced at the clock ticking down the seconds I had left. Twenty seconds, Tate. You can do it. One chance. One chance. I kept my speed, building it faster and faster.

I'd tried it. Practiced it for hours, but only landed it once. One single time. You can do it. I flew, gaining speed back and forth, the ticker on the board winding the seconds down as I hit the coping and launched. Then I was in the air. I was spinning. Once, twice, then the last half. My deck came down straight and true, and I grinned as I sped down the vert. The nine hundred. I'd landed the nine hundred. I'd just knocked on heaven's gate, and it had opened.

I kicked the board out from under me and slid on my knees to the center of the vert, overcome, raising my arms as the crowd went nuts. Shit, they didn't go nuts, they ROARED. The whole place shook.

I looked up to my family's section, and Mom was bawling her head off and Indy was spasming wildly as my dad leaned toward him, no doubt asking what in the hell I'd just done to cause a commotion. I glanced to the side of the vert, and every pro skater stood there, some looking at me like I was a freak while others clapped. A replay of it rolled on the big screen.

The announcer screamed disbelief at an amateur pulling

a run like that, then corrected himself, calling me a pro. Corey Norton stood on the platform staring daggers at me. I stood, and Sid and Pipe slid down the vert, hugging me and clapping my shoulders. Piper screamed in my ear that I'd outdone every pro on the circuit. "None of them yanked a nine hundred, man!!! None! HOLY SHIT!"

I looked at the screen, watching the slow-motion replay. I had done it. I'd done it all. And as I walked from the deck, Corey Norton left his board on the platform—his run still yet to be announced—and walked down the stairs and left the arena. Some things, I thought with a smile, were better than punching a guy out. I looked up at Stick, who grinned, and gave him the thumbs-up.

CHAPTER FORTY-ONE

Fifteen minutes later, after the scores of the pros were announced, all three crews, minus Corey, stood on the platform with the vice president of Flying Gecko Skateboards while the announcer declared Team Hole in the Wall the winners of the amateur competition. With Corey bailing on his crew, they'd had no chance of winning.

I won the Individual, too. The VP of Flying Gecko Skateboards leaned over to me as the crowd thundered. "Keep that up and you'll be a star, young man. We'll be seeing each other soon."

Then it was over. We met Mom, Dad, Indy, Mitch, and Badger at the access door, and Mom slung her arms around me, almost strangling me. Dad clapped me on the shoulder, and Indy grinned. "You did it, dude. You really did it."

I looked at him. "You could have, too."

He shook his head. "No, Tate, I couldn't have. Maybe the nine hundred on a great day, but to pull a line like that without a flaw, no. Not a chance."

I smiled. I'd done it, and if I kept at it, I knew I could do it again. I had a chance now. "Flying Gecko, Indy. I can't believe it."

He smiled. "I can believe it. You're going to hook me up with some swag, right?"

"You got it." We walked out to the concourse, and there, at the top of the landing, stood Kimberly and her parents. She ran down the hall, and as she threw her arms around me, I glanced over her shoulder at her parents. Her dad shuffled uncomfortably and smiled, waving at me. Her mom, with her arms crossed over her chest, clenched her jaw and looked away, ignoring the fact that her daughter was a human being.

Kim kissed my cheek, her eyes shining. "You were *awesome*, Tate. You should have heard the people around us! They went crazy! And now you're a pro! A real pro! That trick thing you did was sooooo cool!"

I grinned, introducing her to Mom and Dad as Mr. Lawson grabbed Mrs. Lawson's hand and yanked her forward. I nodded to him as they reached us, shaking his hand. "I'm Tate. It's nice to meet you, Mr. Lawson."

He smiled, nodding to my board. "It looks like you've got quite a career on your hands. And it's nice to meet you, too." Then he shook hands with my dad and said hello to Mom.

Mrs. Lawson gave an utterly insincere smile, shook hands with my mother, and completely ignored me. I stepped forward. "It's nice to meet you, Mrs. Lawson, and I promise, I won't beat you up and steal your wallet."

Her eyes widened in shock, and Mr. Lawson stifled a smile. Indy laughed outright, and Kimberly giggled, taking my hand. I knew I had a rough road ahead with her pinch-faced mom, but I had a feeling it would be worth it. Back on track, I thought as we walked from the arena. Everything was the way it should be.

Except for one thing.

CHAPTER FORTY-TWO

Mist, just the lightest sprinkle gently coating my face as I skated under the streetlights, sent chills down my spine. It would turn to rain later, I thought, trying to keep my mind from where I was going and what I was about to do. Will. I wouldn't be confronting a guy who wanted to bust it up with me; I'd be confronting a guy who needed my brother dead.

Will thought he'd be seeing Indy. Wrong. He'd be seeing me.

You're an idiot, Tate. You've gone too far this time. Leave it alone for once. It's not your responsibility. I couldn't, though, because he wouldn't go away. This wouldn't fade into nothingness, like when someone was pissed off about some guy dissing him in the cafeteria or knocking him in the hall. There was no anger involved with Will. He needed Indy dead to save his own skin, and it changed things. The hammer would hit harder tonight than it ever had.

And although my dad told me that some things are better talked about than fought over, there was no talking to Will.

There was only action. At least he and I saw things the same way in that respect. Action. Put up or shut up.

Two blocks away from the Monster, I rounded the corner, deep in my thoughts. "Two blocks away. Almost there," I mumbled. "Almost time." I kicked my board up and started walking, and as I did, Will stepped from a doorway, his figure cast in shadow.

He held a pistol, studying me. "You're a pain in my ass. Where is he?"

Panic swept through me. No. This wasn't the place. Not here. I wasn't ready. I looked at Will, clearing my throat and looking at his face, still bruised by my board. "Nice face, asshole. I hope it hurt as much as I enjoyed doing it."

He shrugged. "Two for one, then. You know I'm going to get him after I'm done with you."

I glanced at the store we stood in front of. The China Doll Shop. I nodded my head toward it. "So after all this, I'm going to get smoked in front of a Chinese doll shop. Somehow that fits a pussy like you."

He smiled, enjoying himself. "You always had a mouth."

I sneered. "Did Lucius have a mouth, tough guy?"

He laughed. "Lucius was in the way. Just like you."

"You liked it, didn't you? You got off when you were killing him, huh?"

"The weak die. He was weak," he said, his eyes tightening on me.

I chuckled. "Your uncle told you to scare him away. You killed him for fun."

He shrugged, keeping the pistol on me. "So what if I did? He's gone, and how I got him gone doesn't matter." Then he smiled again. "But yeah, it felt good to cave his head in. Just like it's going to feel good to kill you."

I nodded, the sweat on my forehead mixing with the mist. I braced myself, tensing, then dropped my board, opening my arms. "You're a chickenshit coward, Will. A spineless bitch with a gun to make you look tough."

He smiled, raising the pistol and cocking it.

"You can't take me and you know it. The only reason you need it is because you know I'd kick your ass." I forced a smile. "You're the weak one."

His eyes flashed, and I knew I'd gotten to him. Please. Please let it work. Let there be enough time. He lowered the pistol, uncocking it and putting it in his back pocket. "Tell you what, Tater. You get this gun away from me and we'll see who the pussy is," he said, raising his fists in a fighting stance.

I had my chance, so I took it. I rushed him. I came in swinging like I'd never swung before. Not to win a fight or not get hurt, but to live. To put him down. My fists were pistons.

My first left caught him in the ribs, and my right, with my entire upper body pivoting to put as much force behind it as possible, nailed him square on the eye socket. He flew back, falling to one knee.

Blood seeped from his eye, and in a flash, he flew into me, catching me on the ear with a solid right. I couldn't believe it. The guy could take a punch like nobody I'd seen, and he hit just as hard. Stars flashed in front of my eyes, and then I was being pummeled, his fists hammering me.

I tasted blood and we stood toe to toe, beating the living shit out of each other. No dancing, no jabbing, no dodging, just whaling on each other like we were meat-filled punching bags. Ribs, kidneys, ears, eyes, over and over again we went at each other, each refusing to back off. And it hurt. God did it hurt. I actually felt one of my ribs crack.

Desperate, I lunged in and landed a huge forearm to his eye again, this time accompanied by the sick crunch of his cheekbone fracturing, and he reeled, falling to his knees and reaching for his pistol. I lunged after him. "HURRY UP!" I screamed, grappling with him, trying to keep him from the pistol as pain and fatigue coursed through my body. My face was a bloody mess, the front of my shirt plastered with blood.

On his hands and knees with me on top of him, my arm pinioned around his neck as I tried to pull him back, he twisted, driving his elbow into my cracked rib. I howled, paralyzed, unable to breathe as I fell to the side. The pain was so piercing I almost blacked out, and the next thing I knew, he had the gun in his hands. On his knees, panting, half his face covered in blood, his broken cheekbone grotesquely swollen under the glow of the streetlights, he raised the pistol.

No words, just insanity. I groaned, lying on the ground, huge steel pincers jabbing over and over again into my lung as I breathed. I knew I was dead. Detective Connelly and the police had been waiting on the other side of the park. I wheezed into the hidden wire taped to my chest, wondering if they even knew where I was. I'd hinted about the China Doll Shop when Will had stepped from the shadows, and I hoped to God they'd heard it. *"Hurry. Please."*

Five feet away, Will cocked the pistol, aiming it at my head. His eyes drove into mine like red-hot irons, with no feeling, no anger, just an indifferent and rock-hard intensity that shot straight through me like a knife. I watched as his fingers tightened on the grip. I groaned, looking away, the last tendril of fear spiraling through my gut only to be replaced with resignation. I would die here.

The shot rang out, echoing against the buildings, and my eyes flew open. Blood blossomed on Will's shoulder, and he crumpled, the gun clattering to the pavement. I lay back, staring at the blackness of the sky. I heard running footsteps. A police officer kicked Will's pistol away, then knelt at his side, spinning him on his back, smashing a knee between his shoulder blades, and cuffing him.

Then I passed out.

EPILOGUE

The broken rib punctured my lung when Will drove his elbow into me that last time, and I was in the hospital for three days to make sure my lung didn't collapse. I coughed up blood for two days, and I've got to say it was the worst pain I've ever felt in my life.

But it was done. Will was being charged with first-degree murder and attempted first-degree murder, and he was going away for a long time.

When I was in the hospital, I had two surprise visitors. The first was Ms. Potter. She'd taken heat for helping me, but she explained to me that sometimes taking heat was worth it. She'd taught me a lot. There *were* different ways to do the right thing, but I also realized that not getting yourself into bad situations in the first place was as important as doing the right thing. My brawling days were over. I'd seen that it only led to more fighting, and it wasn't worth risking my life. My path had changed, and Ms. Potter had helped me see that there were different ways to fight.

The second person was Detective Connelly. He knocked, then walked in, dressed in his detective suit. I groaned. "You're not going to arrest me, are you?"

He actually smiled, then shook his head. "I told you that day at the park that my son skates." He paused. "This morning he told me he saw some street skater from Spokane on ESPN, blowing the world away with his tricks." A moment passed, and he handed me a piece of paper and a pen. "His name is Chance. Do you mind? He'd be thrilled."

I wrote him a note, then signed my name.

Connelly tucked it in his pocket. "Good luck, Tate. Stay out of trouble." Then he was gone.

A week later, Mom, Dad, and I, with my ribs still taped, sat in the front row of the Lewis and Clark auditorium and watched as Indy Brooks accepted the second-place award in the Greater Spokane Area Young Writers Competition. For "Stealing Home." Of course Mom bawled her eyes out. The crew sat next to us. Sid farted.

Indy received a one-thousand-dollar scholarship to Eastern Washington University as part of his award. He stayed in school, too, even though he hated every minute of it, except for Mr. Halvorson's English class. By the end of the year, Indy wrote and handed in sixteen short stories about whatever he wanted to write about.

When Dad saw the four A's and one B on Indy's report card, tears glistened in his eyes. And he kept his word, too. Anytime Indy had an issue, Dad would calmly talk to him about it, or he'd ask Mom to handle it. He read everything Indy wrote, too. They actually started getting along, even though Indy would occasionally come home stoned and Dad would get pissed and walk away until he could talk.

Indy's working on quitting the smoke entirely, but I don't know what will happen. You might be able to change Indy a bit, but you can't take the Indy out of Indy. He's a rebel, and he'll always be one.

The crew sort of broke up, but we're still close. Stick started hanging around, too, which was cool because he's really cool. Corey skulks around, being an asshole, but I don't care anymore. I'm on a circuit right now, and I'm doing all right. Middle of the pack, I guess, but traveling on Flying Gecko's nickel. Oh yeah, I was featured in a skate mag last month when I took third in a competition in Arizona. I won three thousand dollars. Me. Tate Brooks. Ha. Maybe I can be something, huh?

The craziest thing is that with all the traveling I'm doing, Indy goes to school more than I do. Irony rules the ironic.

Kim and I are still together, and I actually sort of love her. Okay, I do love her. But don't tell. My tough, cool skater-pro party-guy rep would be ruined.

Indy and I skate with the crew occasionally, but he's changed. He's grown up, I guess. He still has that sense of humor and recklessness about him, but he's more serious. He loves writing. He wants to make a career out of it. He told me Mr. Halvorson is trying to get him accepted into college courses next year, and he's jacked about it. He's been published twice in local mags, too.

I guess having a purpose makes a difference. For both of

us. I always thought Indy would live and die on a skateboard and that I'd fade out of it, but things don't always turn out the way you think. I also believe that Mr. Halvorson, the guy who slammed Indy into the locker that day, saved his life. Some rules, I suppose, are meant to be broken for the right reason.

ACKNOWLEDGMENTS

George Nicholson of Sterling Lord Literistic, my friend and agent, thank you for your integrity and wisdom. Erica Silverman, it goes without saying . . . brilliance at work. My editor, Erin Clarke, Knopf/Random House, you're awesome. Thanks go to Joan Slattery for seeing value in this story. Frank Oberst, thank you for guiding me through school policy and showing what a caring teacher would risk for a student. And as with all of my work, it wouldn't be possible without my wife, Kim.

NOTE FROM THE AUTHOR

IT'S NOT THE RULES YOU FOLLOW,

IT'S HOW YOU FOLLOW THEM.